AF586455

BEYOND BOUNDARIES

Volume 1 2023

BEYOND BOUNDARIES

Volume 1 2023

A Manitoba Writers' Guild Anthology
For
The Dave Williamson Short Story
Competition

Edited by Lori Gaudet

Copyright 2023 Manitoba Writers' Guild Inc.

Manitoba Writers' Guild
Artspace
100 Arthur Street
Winnipeg, MB R3B 1H3

Content printed under license and with permission from the Authors/Creators
Return to Chrysalis ©2023 Bruce Cinnamon
TEOTWAWKI ©2023 Rowan McCandless
Sketches ©2023 Gaylene Dutchyshen
Legend of the Magpie: An Original Métis Story ©2023 Clarence Merle Klyne
The Redhead ©2023 Sharon McInnes
The Other Side of the Map ©2023 Eleonore Schönmaier
On the Edge of My Couch ©2023 Thila Varghese

Photographs reproduced with consent of authors and judges.

Cover Art and Design by Katherine Westwood

Issued in print & electronic formats:
ISBN: 978-0-9692525-9-7

No part of this book may be used or reproduced in form or by any means, including electronic or mechanical, or by any information storage and retrieval system, in any manner whatsoever without the prior written permission of the Manitoba Writers' Guild, except in the case of brief quotations embedded in reviews.

Printed and bound in Canada by PrintoPro Press.

Financial assistance provided by the Manitoba Arts Council.

Table of Contents

The Dave Williamson Short Story Competition

Introduction

By Dave Williamson

More people should read, especially those who would like to write. Of those who do read, many do not read short stories. Yet the short story can be and often is the most enjoyable form of fiction. In fact, whereas the novel is defined as a long work of fiction with flaws, the short story can be perfect.

Canada's own Alice Munro is regarded by many as one of the best short story writers in the world. There are of course many Canadian writers, like Carol Shields and Margaret Atwood, who are best known for their novels, but they too have written fine short stories.

Years ago, Canada's centennial, Expo 67, did much to stimulate the arts, and especially Canadian literature. Regional publishers popped up across the country and, in Manitoba, Winnipeg's Joan Parr started Queenston House, bringing out its first book in 1974, a collection of short stories called Winnipeg Stories. The opening selection was "Courting in 1957," my first-ever short story. Meanwhile, the CBC was also stimulating local arts, and CBWT asked me if I'd like to turn the story into a half-hour TV play, and I did. After that, I wrote three more produced TV scripts—see what a short story can lead to?

Other regional publishers appeared and local writers benefitted. In the early '80s, those writers saw a reason to get together and share information as well as promote their writing. They were anxious to show local readers that serious American writers like Anne Tyler and John Updike and trash writers like Harold Robbins and Jacqueline Susann were not the only people who could tell a good yarn. So began the Manitoba Writers' Guild. By the time I was president, we were meeting with like-minded groups in Saskatchewan, Minnesota, North Dakota and

South Dakota. And we knew it was time to create and publicize an award for the Best Manitoba Book of the Year.

McNally Robinson Booksellers were only too happy to help us, and they donated the $1000 prize. That of course led over the next few years to a number of prizes, and the presentation event was taken over by a group dedicated to the annual awards.

In the last couple of years, the Guild has become even more proactive in encouraging and helping Manitoba writers. The Guild is creating events to bring writers together and is publishing a semi-monthly on-line newsletter that is chock full of information. A Youth Writing Group has been established to help Manitobans at an early age. Launching of members' books is a priority. And now the Guild has introduced a short story contest—open to writers across Canada.

At the March 1, 2023 deadline, there were 96 entries. Well-qualified judges have gone over them and picked the winners. Congratulations to all entrants for proving that you believe in the short story. Congratulations to the winners, who are presented here in this anthology, which the Guild intends to present every year at this time and help promote short story excellence.

Welcome to Beyond Boundaries Volume 1 2023

By Andy Dutfield

In 2022, The Manitoba Writers' Guild (MWG) discussed the need to update and upsize our seasonal short story contests to capture the attention of more Manitoba writers. We wanted to create a competition with broader appeal not only across the province but also across the country.

The Dave Williamson Short Story Competition evolved from these discussions. We are heartened by and delighted with the diverse range of stories our jurors have received during this inaugural year, coming from as far west as Nanaimo, BC, as far east as Conception Bay, Newfoundland, as far north as the Yukon, and throughout Manitoba from the Interlake and Whiteshell to the lush southern farmlands.

Seeking to preserve and honour the history of the Guild, we chose distinguished local author Dave Williamson as our Honorary Patron. Not only was he a founding member of the Guild, but he also founded and developed the nationally acknowledged Creative Communications program at Red River College and served as Chair of the Writers' Union of Canada 1992-93. Dave Williamson, thank you for allowing us to use your name.

To attract more writers throughout Manitoba and across the country, we boosted our prize levels. Members chipped in with generous donations to enable us to reach our new goals. On behalf of the Guild, I thank them for their generosity. With sincere gratitude, I also want to acknowledge the support of the Manitoba Arts Council, which guaranteed that the competition would be able to proceed as planned.

The competition required extensive promotion and countless hours of professional planning and execution, followed by thorough juried evaluation. I thank Sharon Hamilton,

Alex Dawson and their team for all their efforts. You will find a comprehensive listing of the jurors in a few pages and a complete listing of our members and volunteers who worked on this projected in the Acknowledgements at the end of this volume.

And finally, we come to the culmination of the competition, Beyond Boundaries, which captures the essence of what we have tried to achieve in this inaugural year. We have stretched our vision beyond its usual boundaries; we have sought participation beyond our usual boundaries, and our authors have taken us to different literary worlds beyond our usual boundaries. Whether you are a prize winner, an honourable mention, a proud family member, a friend, or somebody interested in reading talented writers, the Guild hopes you enjoy this book.

WINNERS

FIRST PLACE

Return to Chrysalis
Bruce Cinnamon

SECOND PLACE

TEOTWAWKI
Rowan McCandless

THIRD PLACE

Sketches
Gaylene Dutchyshen

HONOURABLE MENTIONS
(alphabetical)

The Legend of Magpie: An Original Métis Story
Clarence Merle Klyne

The Redhead
Sharon McInnes

The Other Side of the Map
Eleonore Schönmaier

On the Edge of My Couch
Thila Varghese

BRUCE CINNAMON

Bruce Cinnamon is a writer and editor from Edmonton, Alberta. His first novel, *The Melting Queen*, was published by NeWest Press in 2019. He is currently working on his second novel, a multiverse-spanning adventure addressing ecological collapse, queer liberation, and postcolonial justice. When he's not writing fiction, Bruce works as a communications officer for the North Atlantic Treaty Organization (NATO).

* *Photo by Neil Siviter*

Return to Chrysalis

Bruce Cinnamon

Like most extravagant homosexuals, I fled my rural shitstain of a hometown with the traumatized haste of a refugee. After high school, I flitted from city to city, trading up through larger and larger metropolises before finally alighting in the biggest, farthest city I could find. I feasted my way through a smorgasbord of earthly delights, indulging in all the sinful human appetites that had built up within me like champagne locked away behind a mile-high dam (part of me had worried that all those years of shame and self-mutilation had permanently flattened my fizz, but the effervescence only fed itself once freed). No matter how drafty my shoebox apartments, no matter how many auditions I did and jobs I failed to book, I always could look at myself in the mirror every morning and say: *you're here. You did it. Look how far you've come.*

So it was with no great pleasure that I returned to my toxic little town when an unexpected global pandemic started closing all borders and cancelled all my work. My mom called me, insisting that the world was ending and her only child *should at least do his mother this one last favour goddammit.*

My parents and I have had a decisively colourless relationship since my great migration. They're not religious nutbags or Facebook-radicalized cultists. But they also knew exactly who and what I was for years before I came out, and though they didn't kick me out or try to have me tortured into heterosexuality, they also made no effort to stand up for me or shield me from their neighbours. And I remember every moment. Being not-as-bad-as-the-average-bigot is a low bar to clear, and it gets lower every year. So the connection we maintain is bloodless, varying between formal and frosty.

But then again, I was broke. And I was worried about getting a deadly respiratory illness in a country without public healthcare. So, against my better judgement, I agreed to spend the end of the world back in the town of my birth. Home sweet home.

They say that Paris would be heaven on earth, if not for all the Parisians. Over many years of separation and decontamination, I've come to think the same about my hometown. It has all the necessary ingredients of a charming small town: a diner that serves surprisingly great breakfast food (although everything else on the menu is clearly fresh from the freezer and microwave); a crumbling ornate cinema that is probably a money laundering front for a drug ring (it somehow stays in business despite charging two bucks for everything); a vintage candy shop with floor-to-ceiling shelves of giant glass jars full of sweets (where I developed my lifelong sour tooth by being the only kid who loved their mouth-melting lemon gobstoppers). In short, it has all the nostalgic charm of an idyllic 1950s suburb. Unfortunately, its residents have all the politics and prejudices of that era as well.

In the city, everyone always said the same thing when I told them where I was from: *thank god you escaped that shithole, good for you for getting yourself out of there*. It never bothered me when I heard it from other queer émigrées – they knew exactly what I had gone through to get there, the hungry days and cold nights and humiliating jobs. But with people born in the city, you could always hear the slight subtext of *you must be so grateful, you're so lucky to be here* in their voices. Yes, I was grateful. Yes, I was lucky. But even though I hate my hometown with a burning passion, part of me always thought *your city ain't shit compared to mine*. You don't appreciate clean, fresh air and pure, glacier-fed water until you go for a run in a smog-choked city and your throat burns for days. You don't appreciate seeing a million stars every night, with occasional guest appearances by the northern lights, until you live in a city whose lights never go out. Of course I was happy to have escaped. But part of me always thought of myself not as a permanent migrant to the metropolis, but as a prince-in-exile, waiting patiently for my kingdom to liberate itself from various tyrannies and catch up to a more relaxed, liberated world. Waiting for the small-minded backwater to make penance for its sins. To apologize. To finally deserve me.

My return came sooner than I expected, and for different reasons. After a long day of endless flights and transfers to increasingly smaller and shabbier airports, I was home. I gave my mom a stiff hug and my dad a sharp nod and then I settled into a pattern that came to define my time there.

I woke up as early as I could, in that little pause right before the sun rises, and went for a long run every morning. I've had a love-hate (mostly hate) relationship with my body ever since it failed to bloom into the tired G.I. Joe stereotype of masculinity I simultaneously despised and desired. Running has always at least let me feel some degree of control over my body. I ran past St. Christopher's church (where I sat every Sunday begging Jesus to make me straight), past my high school (where I sat for three years waiting for the long slog of standardized education to end), past the boarded-up remains of the video store (where I sat most weekday evenings renting out shitty action movies to men and shitty romcoms to women, furtively eyeing up the male figures on the DVDs in the walled-off porno section as I vacuumed after closing). The town was rotting away, and I was thriving. Running past the sad, small structures only reinforced how proud and tall I had become.

After some time (it may have been days, it may have been weeks – time had imploded during Miss Rona), I noticed that someone else was also running through town at this ungodly hour. I saw him going up and down the empty streets, never quite crossing paths with me, but popping in and out of my periphery most mornings. He looked around my age, so he was probably another prodigal son – no shade, but the young men who'd stuck around were not the type to go running at the crack of dawn, if ever. We kept a respectful distance from each other (I assumed he also held sacred the meditative solitude of running, or maybe he was just following the public health measures more strictly than most people did out here).

The weeks went by and I got used to him being there, and even felt somewhat disappointed on days when I didn't see him. Things started to open up back in the city – the world hadn't ended, although some of my arguments with my parents came close to triggering an apocalypse or two – and I plotted my departure. I had a few friends I could crash with, rich kids who had also grown tired of staying back home (probably sick of being doted on by overly attentive parents). I'd scraped together some money from a few random voice-acting jobs I'd landed (and flat-out refused to pay my dad rent when he floated the idea one day). So I booked my ticket and started counting down the days.

The day I was due to leave, I went for one last farewell run. Rather than running straight home as usual, I decided to stretch beside the grandiose fountain in front of city hall. I'd always loved this inappropriately lavish fountain, with its gold curlicues and random pastiche of mythological figures. It felt like something from a different town, one with more ambition, more whimsy, more tolerance for bizarrerie. The mayor and councillors who ordered it built were embroiled in some kind of miniature expense scandal at the time for how much it cost, and all of them resigned midway through construction. It was never finished, and never hooked up to water, instead becoming a catch-all receptacle for dead leaves, empty beer cans, and the ill-advised wishing coins of townsfolk desperate for a lottery win. I think it was supposed to be a memorial to something, but some drunk kids stole the plaque and it was never replaced. The central plinth at the top of the fountain was left empty – I'd always imagined that they would one day put a golden statue of me up there, when I was famous. They'd ask me to come home and unveil it, and I'd consider it.

"Good morning."

He'd run up beside me without me noticing. I must've looked offended at the intrusion, because he held up his hands like a zookeeper trying to calm a pissed-off peacock.

"Sorry, didn't mean to startle you. And don't worry, I'll stay more than two metres away. Just figured I should finally say hi. I've seen you out here for a while."

He was tall, dark, and handsome in a generic way that would've won him the lead role in dozens of shows and movies (ugh). His eyes were brown like those square caramels they used to throw at parades until some kid got hit in the eye and they stopped throwing candy. They caught the light of the morning sun. He seemed suspiciously happy and intensely focused on my face. Maybe he wanted to pound me in the bushes behind city hall (but maybe I was just thinking that because I'm a big slut in the middle of a pandemic-induced sex drought, with vanishingly few opportunities to jerk off in a house my parents never seemed to leave).

"Hi," I said back. "How was your run?"

"Decent," he said, wiping the sweat from his forehead like a model in a Nike ad. "Mind if I stretch with you?"

"Sure, no worries."

He proceeded to do a hamstring stretch at the other end of the fountain, showing off a pretty decent set of legs.

"So I don't want to sound like a creep or a stalker or anything, but I know who you are." He flashed me a semi-apologetic smile. "I saw that Netflix show you were in. You were really good."

"Thanks," I said awkwardly. I'd never known how to respond when people say they've seen me in something, and here it felt especially strange – like when you invite all your friends from different social circles to your birthday party and they start comparing notes about the different versions of yourself. "I've mostly just done theatre and some dance stuff. Cruise ships, that sort of thing. My agent put me up for it and I guess they liked me."

"That's so cool. I can't wait for the next season."

"They cancelled it. Everything shut down and they decided not to bring that one back."

"Oh. I'm sorry. That sucks, man. Still, amazing that you got to work on it. I'm sure you'll get some other great parts when this whole thing is over."

I watched as the wind picked up a bright gold candy wrapper from the fountain and carried it up into the air and out of sight.

"What do you do?" I asked him.

"I work in finance. Not nearly as exciting, but it pays the bills. I'm teleworking now."

I straightened up from my quad stretch and crossed my arms.

"I'm sorry if this is a rude question, but if you still have a job, why are you here?"

He looked at me for a moment, a shadow on his face like a cloud crossing a field, then went back to focusing on his stretch.

"My dad died," he said eventually. "Not from COVID, just regular old cancer. I'm here to help my mom with stuff."

"Oh. Shit. I'm sorry."

"Thank you."

He finished his last stretch and turned to face the town.

"Do you want to walk for a bit? I don't have to start work until 9:00 or so. It's flexible."

I studied his face, trying to figure him out. Was he a fuck-starved ho like me? Or a star-struck bro who wanted a story to tell (not that anyone would care)? Or just a dude facing down endless months of loneliness like everyone else? There was something familiar in his eyes – a heavy door with bright light shining through the keyhole.

"Sure. Let's walk."

We went in circles around the town, chatting about all the things that had changed, how much smaller everything seemed, conversation so conventional that I wished we could just chat about the weather instead. We walked past the post office, past the musty old library and the gleaming new hockey arena.

He was taller than me by a head, but I noticed that he slouched his shoulders. I held my head high.

"We went to school together, by the way," he said after a while. "I'm Matt. Matt Clark."

"I'm sorry," I said. "I don't remember you."

"That's fine," he said immediately. "We didn't really know each other. I was in grade ten when you were in grade twelve. My brother Kevin was in your class."

I looked at the murals painted on the walls of the arena – big, beefy boys playing hockey, ready to slam each other into the boards.

"I remember Kevin."

Eventually, we made our way to the railroad tracks at the edge of town, where the trains called out their wistful songs to each other in the night.

"Well, I go this way," I said, pointing down the street toward my parents' house. "I should probably get going."

"Nice," he said, rocking back and forth on the balls of his feet. "Uh, would you want to go for a run together some time? I'm not sure what your average pace is. But it's nice to have a motivation buddy."

"That would be cool," I said. "But I'm actually leaving in a few hours and I still haven't packed."

I felt a lingering tension between us, a familiar uncertainty and expectation emanating from his body. I stood there, waiting to see how it would play out.

"Cool," he said. "Um, not to be weird or anything, but I just had to say, I really looked up to you back then, in high school. You were really… you weren't like anyone else."

I smirked, held his gaze for that well-practised extra millisecond.

"Why would I want to be like anyone else?"

He smiled, blushing a little and looking away.

"Good point," he said. "Uh, would you want to connect on Insta or something?"

"Sure," I said. "My handle is just my name. I'll be easy to find. If you haven't creeped my profile already."

I gave him a wolf's grin, savouring the rosé rising up his neck. Oh prairie boy, you still have miles to go.

"Nice," he said, staring out over the fields. "I'll look you up."

He seemed to steel himself a little before looking back at me.

"Maybe we can reconnect when things go back to normal," he said with ham-fisted casualness. "If we're ever in the same place, I mean."

"I think it'll be years before anything is back to normal," I said drily.

"Don't say that," he groaned. "I don't think I can stand another month of this."

I looked him in the eye and this time he held my gaze.

"Yes, you can," I said quietly. "As long as you have to."

He nodded slowly. He was still on his journey, just like the rest of us. But he understood. Over years and years, he had learned a strength that few possessed. A rare patience in an age of haste.

The story of my life in my hometown was a story of waiting. Waiting to stop being different from everyone else, when I thought I was the problem. Waiting for things to get better, when I realised that I was perfect just the way I was and everyone else was the problem. And when I realized that neither of those things would happen, just waiting to get out. Doing my time in the same pointless little routines. Forcing myself to believe that someday, in the distant future, I wouldn't be trapped anymore. I could go anywhere I liked, be anyone I liked, fuck anyone I liked.

And I did. Almost as soon as I was away from there, I made true friends for the first time. I felt happy. I felt like a real, full person, not just a hollow shell going through the motions. I was free.

So many straight people I know have been emotionally destroyed by this pandemic. But not my queer friends and lovers. Not me.

I've lived through this whole situation before. I've had to spend years in isolation, keeping a safe distance from everyone around me. I've had to put on a mask to survive. I've had to wait, spinning my wheels, trusting that a better life was just over the horizon – that I would emerge from that long grey hibernation and spread my resplendent wings.

It's hard to be back in that space. It sucks. But no matter how long it lasts, I know that I'll come out of it stronger. I did before. And I will again.

ROWAN MCCANDLESS

Rowan McCandless writes from Treaty 1 territory. A finalist for the 2022 Governor General's Literary Award in nonfiction, Rowan's debut memoir, *Persephone's Children: A Life in Fragments* also co-won the Eileen McTavish Sykes Award for Best First Book (2022) and was a finalist in the nonfiction category. Her award-winning writing has appeared in various anthologies and journals. Long listed for the Journey Prize, winner of the Constance Rooke CNF prize, gold winner with the National Magazine Awards, Rowan is the Creative Nonfiction editor with The Fiddlehead magazine. Follow Rowan on Twitter (@rowanmccandless),

Instagram (rowanmccandlesswrites) or online (rowanmccandlesswrites.com).

* *Photo by Tessa Vallittu*

TEOTWAWKI

Rowan McCandless

I hate to break it to you, but it's a fact, plain and simple; in this world, it's survival of the fittest. Another simple fact? Jamie Barnes can't climb a rope worth shit, and our jerk-off of a gym teacher knows it.

"Come on, Barnes," Mr. C. says, glancing at his Timex wristwatch. "Time's a-wasting and I'm not getting any younger."

Jamie's face turns beet red as he white-knuckles the rope suspended from the gymnasium's ceiling. His arms shake like Mom's Jell-O ribbon salad. He's giving it all he's got—not that it matters, cuz I'm pretty sure if he straightened his legs his feet would still brush the floor.

"I can't," Jamie says, twirling in circles like one of Dad's Old Spice soap-on-a-ropes.

Mr. C. removes the Bic pen attached to his clipboard, starts poking poor Jamie with the capped end like he's the Pillsbury Doughboy.

"Don't"—poke— "you dare"—poke— "let go of that"—poke, jab— "rope," Mr. C. says.

Things go from bad to worse, cuz the higher Jamie reaches on the rope, the lower his gym shorts slide down.

My best friend, Charlie, elbows me in the side. “His ass crack’s showing.”

Some of the boys in our grade seven gym class grunt like little piggies. The Ashleys start giggling. Ashley H. laughs the loudest.

Geez Louise, now Jamie’s crying. He’s got snot dangling from his nostrils like bungee cords.

“Pathetic, Barnes,” Mr. C. says. “Absolutely pathetic.”

Dad says some people are like that—you know, pathetic. They’re weak-willed and soft, and that makes them a target. Still, it doesn’t seem fair that Jamie’s gotta suffer just cuz he’s cursed with the same sorry physical constitution as the rest of his family.

“This is bullshit,” I whisper to Charlie.

“Something you’d like to share, Westerberg?” Mr. C. says.

I shake my head. No.

“Didn’t think so.”

I stare at the crisscross of lines on the hardwood floor and can’t help wondering: Would Mr. C. and the rest of the class be a whole lot nicer to Jamie if they knew what I know? That TEOTWAWKI’s coming. Dad says it could be any day now.

The

End

Of

The
World
As
We
Know
It

"Come on, Barnes. Before it's Christmas."

But Mr. C. doesn't know TEOTWAWKI's coming, any more than he knows last Christmas could very well have been exactly that—the honest-to-goodness last one celebrated on the planet. So, I guess Jamie's just SOL in more ways than one.

Except for Charlie, who's been my best friend since kindergarten, they're all SOL. They just don't know it yet.

There's this thud as Jamie lands ass-first on the mat.

"Can I go see the school nurse?" he says, cupping and cradling his hands cuz of some nasty rope burns.

"What are you? Some kind of baby? Suck it up, Buttercup." Mr. C. looks my way. "Westerberg! Show Barnes how it's done."

I take a step forward.

Jamie takes two steps back, blowing onto his palms like he's trying to snuff out lit candles on a birthday cake. He's got this pleading look on his face, like I'm the only one who can save him and his reputation from total annihilation. But what can I do? I'm not about to be anyone's target, cuz I'm not weak—or soft.

I grab the rope. It's thick and coarse in my hands. I loop it under my knee, over my foot.

"Go, go, Westerberger," Charlie cheers from the sidelines.

Dad would have a major conniption if he knew I told Charlie about TEOTWAWKI, but I know Charlie wouldn't betray us and I can't imagine surviving the end of the world without him. I'd warn everyone like I did Charlie (well, maybe not Mr. C., and if I'm honest, I'm kinda on the fence when it comes to saving the Ashleys, especially Ashley H.), but I can't. Dad says we gotta keep it and my visions on the q.t. Says, "The last thing we need, when the GD shit hits the GD fan, is a bunch of pie-eyed, shit-scared townies after our supplies."

Mr. C. blows the whistle around his neck.

I pinch the rope between my feet and look up at the rafters, testing my weight and my hold on the line.

I start my climb. Find my rhythm. Superstar.

Dad says, when the time comes we gotta be ready. Only the strong will survive. So, I've been working out, big time. I can do 98 push-ups, 117 sit-ups, and 143 star jumps. No joke. I'm serious. I'm not lying. And I'm sure as hell not some pathetic cry-baby like you-know-who.

From the top of the rope, I look down at the Grade 1-ers tossing bean bags at one another in barefoot gym while Mrs. Rempel's Grade 4 class plays murderball.

Mr. C. gathers everyone's attention like a barker at a carnival. He says, "Ladies and gentlemen, our Mr. Barnes has just been shown up by a girl. Do me a favour, Barnes, and get out of my sight."

Jamie starts his walk of shame toward the exit.

I wave at Charlie but get no response, cuz he's too busy making googly eyes at Ashley H., who's the first girl in our grade seven class to smoke cigarettes, and sneak booze out of a parents' liquor cabinet, and five finger discount Bonne Belle makeup from Selkirk's five and dime store. She also looks a whole lot different wearing our school gym uniform than the rest of the girls in our class; the infamous greenie, the bloomer-bottomed bane of my very existence. I'm still flat as a board and skinny as a rail. Ma says, good things come to those who wait, and I'll grow into my beauty. That I'm just a late bloomer like she was. But what's the point of being a late bloomer if the world is coming to an end?

Ashley H. touches Charlie on the arm, and my temples start throbbing, my ears start ringing, and pinpoints of light cascade from the rafters like shooting stars.

Jamie's almost at the exit when I sense this blast shake the gymnasium.

"Run, Jamie. Run," I shout but all he does is turn around and flip me the bird before pulling the gym door open.

A tidal wave of heat roars into the gym, followed by a river of fire engulfing everything and everyone in its path. The smell of sulfur, of smoke, of burning flesh makes me want to puke. Jamie looks like the Human Torch. *Snap. Crackle. Pop.* He's toast.

Flames spread across the hardwood floor, lick the gym bleachers.

"Run!" I tell them. "Fucking run!"

Mr. C. melts like a wax mannequin. So do all the Ashleys. Especially Ashley H.

I close my eyes, trying to shut out the destruction, but there's no way to rid my nose of the smell, the images stuck in my brain. I feel like bawling, but I can't. Cuz bawling's for wusses—and Dad says there's no room for wusses, before, during, or after the apocalypse.

"Way to go, Westerburger!" Charlie says.

I squeeze my lids as tight as I can. "I'm sorry, Charlie. I'm sorry." I hear screams of torment. Howling. The sound in my ears blares like sirens, like ringing bells, the recess bell, like static, like the high-pitched nasal whine of the secretary's voice coming over the PA system. "Will Cassie Westerberg please come down to the principal's office?"

There's laughter down below.

"Zip it!" Mr. C. says. "Westerberg, get down here!"

I open my eyes. Everyone's staring at me.

"Today, Westerberg!"

I climb down and land feet-first on the mat. Mr. C.'s looks at me like I'm some kind of nut job. So do the Ashleys. Especially Ashley H., with her nose in the air like I've got major B.O. or something.

"Office." Mr. C says.

"You okay?" Charlie asks.

"I'm fine."

Mr. C chucks a dodgeball at Charlie's head, tells him to mind his own bee's wax and for me to get a move on.

Like I said, it's survival of the fittest.

*

There's a lot of things I'm going to miss on account of the apocalypse.

Three things I'm going to miss:

- Saturday Night Live and Mary Katherine Gallagher, Superstar.
- The Montreal Canadiens.
- And my mom if she winds up leaving us for good for Mr. Saunders, who owns the local Dutch Maid ice-cream parlour.

Three things I'm not gonna miss? Besides Mr. C? Ha, ha.

- Mr. Saunders.
- The Ashleys. Especially Ashley H.
- And Mrs. Gordon, the School Nurse, who's the reason I got called down to the principal's office.

Good thing Dad warned me about interrogation. That's why I practice every day. With sticks. With fire. With punches to the gut. Nothing can break me. Mrs. Gordon, the busybody, can sit there and ask me a million questions. See if I care. It's not like I'm gonna answer.

*

During recess, me and Charlie hide out in a corner of the far field next to the crappy baseball diamond. We sit in the tall grass, with our backs leaning against the chain link.

"Gordon still riding your ass?" Charlie says.

"Yeah. She keeps asking how things are at home. Says, my teachers are all concerned cuz I'm distracted in class and my grades are slipping. She says, "It's like you're lost in your own little world, Cassandra."

"Effin busybody," Charlie says.

"No kidding."

"What'd ya tell her?"

I hold my hand under Dad's Zippo lighter. "Nothing," I say. "Not a goddamn thing."

I didn't tell her how Mom has up and left us. How she got tired of waiting around for the Rapture to happen or for Dad to get a real job. I didn't mention that we've got canned goods stockpiled like crazy at home, TP stacked to the ceiling, and enough cans of Klik and cling peaches to last a hundred years.

I sure don't share how Dad wakes me and my little brothers up at all hours of the night to run drills, so he can time how long it takes for us to put on our gas masks and haul ass down to the root cellar. Or that wearing shoes to bed can shave a good forty-seven seconds off your time, which may not sound like much, but could be the difference between making a safe escape or getting you and what's left of your family captured and killed by a band of godless marauders cuz you're nothing but a slowpoke.

Charlie pushes my hand away from the flame. "Jesus," he says. "Enough."

I lie on my back. Charlie lies on the grass beside me.

We watch clouds float by. Listen to the chirp of crickets. Feel the warmth of the sun.

Charlie plucks a blade of switchgrass and makes a whistle out of it.

I reach for the sky, capture clouds between my thumb and fingertip. Let them go.

"Do you know that there's this thing called the ozone layer?" I say to Charlie. "It wraps around the entire planet. You can't see it. It's like, invisible to the naked eye."

He stops whistling.

"It protects every living thing on Earth from what's called UV rays. Rays . . . like in radiation. Right now, there's a hole in the ozone layer that's almost as big as Antarctica."

Charlie yawns. Stretches.

"What do you think of Ashley?" he says.

"Ashley? Which Ashley? Ashley C.? Ashley J.? Ashley S.?"

"Ashley H."

I shudder and my face puckers up like I've been sucking on a lemon. "She uses so much junky hair-spray, I bet she's like, personally responsible for half the hole in the ozone layer."

"I dunno. She seems okay."

"Ashley H.. Ashley H.. What's so great about Ashley H.?"

"She seems kinda nice and stuff."

I look at Charlie. "What do you mean . . . and stuff?"

His face reddens. "Forget I said anything."

"Forget you said anything? Charlie, TEOTWAWKI's coming. Do you honestly think Ashley H. is going to know what to do or how to take care of herself?"

Charlie points at a cloud. "Hey" he says. "That one looks like a giant parrot."

"I mean Ashley's so dumb, I bet she doesn't even know how to rig a fishing line or read a compass."

"And over there. That one looks like a dolphin."

"So dumb, I bet she doesn't even know how to build a half-decent hidey-hole. Let alone camouflage it. And shoot a bow and arrow with those polished nails of hers? Forget about it."

"You don't have to be so mean."

"I'm not being mean. I'm being, you know, practical. When the time comes, we have to be ready, Charlie."

"Cassie. Geez, give it a rest. Just cuz bad things happen in this world doesn't mean it's gonna go all kablooey. I mean, it was okay pretending this stuff when we were little, but we're not kids anymore and—"

"Don't let her distract you, Charlie. Don't lose your focus on account of some stupid girl."

"You're a girl."

A marshmallow dragon floats across the sky. It swallows the sun.

I start doing sit-ups.

Charlie holds down my legs. He's got this sad look on his face.

"I'm just trying to look out for you, Charlie."

"I know," he says, with a reassuring smile.

I can tell he feels kinda bad.

"When the time comes," Charlie says. "How do you think it'll happen?"

The dragon breaks apart, scatters in all directions. The sun comes out again.

"Don't know," I tell him. "Could be nukes. Maybe a killer asteroid."

"What about cyborgs? Like in The Terminator."

"Could be. Or maybe some kind of plague. Dad says the government's got secret labs all over the place. That they're cooking up all kinds of batshit crazy diseases."

"How 'bout an alien invasion?"

"Don't be stupid. There's no such thing as aliens."

"How do you know?"

"I know cuz there's no aliens in the Bible, dummy."

Poor Charlie. It's not his fault that his foster-parents are raising him to be a godless heathen.

Airplanes circle like hawks overhead. Paratroopers fall from the sky. There's this shrill shriek of sirens. I stop doing sit-ups. Dig my nails into my wrists.

"Cassie!" Charlie says.

"What?"

"Time's up."

I trade places with Charlie under a blue sky dotted with cotton balls. He's pretty good at sit-ups, but not as good as me.

"Maybe it'll be zombies?" Charlie says.

I nod. I figure I owe him that much.

"Maybe," I say. "You never know."

The bell rings. Recess is over. No more soccer or kickball, skipping double or "What time is it, Mr. Wolf?". No more kindergarteners holding hands, dancing in circles to "Ring Around the Rosie", singing "Ashes. Ashes. We all fall down."

*

At the end of the school day, me and Charlie line up with the rest of the lemmings, waiting on school buses to take us home. Jamie's two rows over, getting a wedgie. For his sake, when the time comes, I hope that it is a zombie apocalypse. His life would probably be a whole lot easier as one of the living dead.

A truck pulls into the parking lot, blasting its horn.

I get this queasy feeling. "What's he doing here?"

"Go," Charlie says. "Don't worry about me."

But I do.

I run over to Dad's pick-up. The cargo area is crammed with blue plastic water barrels. In the back of the extended cab, my little brothers are fast asleep in their car seats. They've got chocolate ice-cream smeared all over their faces.

"I finished some errands. Thought I'd swing by," Dad says.

Errands? More like another bunch of excuses if you ask me. Just so he can cruise up to Dutch Maid's Drive-Thru and beg Mom, who works the take-out window, to come home with him over the microphone. That's the only way she'll talk to him now.

"Get in," Dad says.

I ask about Charlie.

"What about him?"

"Can we give him a ride?"

Dad looks over and shrugs.

I signal Charlie. He bolts from line, and I give him the window seat.

"Thanks for the ride, Mr. Westerberg."

"Uh huh," Dad says, and pops the clutch.

Charlie gets nervous around my father. So, he starts blabbering about all kinds of dumb shit. Dad lights a smoke and turns on the radio. Conversation's over.

Our town's not much to look at. There's a hardware store, a few mom-and-pop shops, a Chinese restaurant, a bunch of beat-up houses, a gas station, and Dutch Maid's Ice-Cream Parlour. Still, it's home and memories, and it makes me sad to think of the place disintegrating beneath a mushroom cloud.

Past the outskirts, it's nothing but weedy poplars, towering pine, and wilderness. We travel a divided highway. The windows are cranked and there's a warm breeze. We pass Smokey the Bear holding a sign saying, *Only You Can Prevent Forest Fires*.

From Smokey's billboard, it's an hour's walk to reach one of Dad's secret spider holes. It's dug as long as Dad is tall, with just enough room to lay down. It's camouflaged real good. I oughta know, cuz I'm the one who helped him spread branches, twigs, and pebbles on top of the plywood covering the trench. Dad's got a network of spider holes, spread out in the woods for miles. They're there in case of emergency. Safe locations for us to go to in case our home gets overrun by bad guys once TEOTWAWKI happens.

We turn down a service road and stop in front of a long gravel driveway.

"Thanks, Mr. Westerberg," Charlie says. He gathers his belongings. Reaches for the door handle.

"I'll see you tomorrow?" he says.

"See you tomorrow," I say. "Promise."

We leave Charlie standing by the side of the road.

Dad says, "Don't go making promises you might not be able to keep."

I focus on Charlie . . . wave until he's nothing but a speck in the distance.

Dad turns off the radio. He lights another smoke.

"You said something to that McAllister boy."

"I—"

"Don't lie to me."

"Charlie promised. He swore on a stack of Bibles that he wouldn't say anything."

"Cassie, blood's thicker than water. And family takes care of their own."

My little brothers start fussing.

"That so? Well then, maybe someone should remind Mom of that."

Dad winces, and I wish I could take back what I just said.

"Charlie's got his own to worry about," Dad says. "You need to understand that. You like to think people are good because of the goodness in you, Cassie. But human beings are a flawed creation. We're selfish and cruel.

And when push comes to shove, I hate to tell you, but that McAllister boy will think nothing of screwing you over."

"You're wrong about Charlie."

"Guess we'll find out."

Dad pulls onto the shoulder. He grabs my bug-out bag from behind the seat. The knapsack's full of supplies and weighs a ton. "You've been a little slow lately. Now's not the time to be slacking off."

"Yes sir."

I sling my bug-out bag over my shoulder.

"Cassie."

"Ya?"

"She's coming back. Your mother knows it's not safe out there. She'll be home soon. I can feel it in my bones."

"Okay."

There's nothing more for me to say. Not out loud anyways. Dad says he married the prettiest girl in town, the woman of his dreams. Mom says she married a dreamer, with a few loose screws in his head. She's not coming back. Not ever. I know cuz that's what she told me, the morning she left with Mr. Saunders. Dad doesn't know about Mr. Saunders, and I don't want to be the one to tell him. I don't want to make Dad sad. Send him free-falling into that deep pit of despair I work so hard to save him from. I don't want Dad to cry. Cuz bawling's for wusses. There's no room for wusses, before during, or after the apocalypse and me and my little brothers really need him around.

I hop out of the truck.

“Chop. Chop,” Dad says. “I’ll see you at home. It’s Klik casserole and peach flambé for supper tonight.”

He drives off.

I’m left breathing gravel dust in the middle of nowhere. I gotta start running. I just don't know where.

GAYLENE DUTCHYSHEN

A short story written for a creative writing course was the spark that inspired Gaylene Dutchyshen's first published novel, *A Strange Kind of Comfort*. It was released in January 2020 by Dundurn Press, Toronto, and was nominated for the Eileen Sykes Best First Novel Award at the Manitoba Book Awards in 2021.

Born in Dauphin and raised in nearby Gilbert Plains, Gaylene was a bookworm who wrote her first novel when she was thirteen. She and her husband Wayne raised three children while operating a large grain and cattle farm in Gilbert Plains.

Gaylene is seeking a publisher for her second novel, *The Third Secret*, and is currently working on a psychological thriller.

Now semi-retired, Gaylene and Wayne enjoy travelling, soaking in the culture and ambience of their destination at outdoor cafes, sipping on the best local wines.

* *Photo by Kelly Michaluk Photography*

Sketches

Gaylene Dutchyshen

Clara has a box she hides from Earl. It is navy blue and smells faintly of rose water, with the gold emblem of the T. Eaton Company embossed on the fitted lid. The box, or rather the lace-edged Egyptian cotton sheets it once held, had been a wedding gift from her Great-Aunt May. Long ago, Clara tucked away the fancy sheets in a trunk until she might have a use for them, but the box, itself, is perfect. In it she collects faces of people she knows on usable squares of brown paper.

She is working on a new sketch now, trying to capture the perfect tilt of a chin, smudging the charcoal pencil strokes with the tip of her finger. Earl doesn't like it when she draws. He caught her at it once when Jolene was not yet in school. With a crazed look in his eyes, he swept her pencils off the table, crumpled and tore up her cherished sketches and tossed them in the wood stove. She watched in horror as flames licked at the edges of her favourite drawing of Jolene, sleeping on the sofa the way she used to, with her thumb in her mouth.

Just then she hears Earl's truck pull up to the house. She shoves the sketch into the box then stuffs the whole works into the cold oven, slamming shut the door.

"Got any more coffee?" He doesn't bother taking off his boots, tracking in cow shit and mud over the floor. He sinks into his chair, picking at a bit of food between his teeth with a dirt-caked nail as he surveys the kitchen. "Been real busy again this morning, I see."

The breakfast dishes are still on the table. The runny egg Jolene failed to sop up with her toast is crusted onto a plate. A freshly-picked basket of soiled eggs sits by the sink, needing to be washed, and a five-gallon pail of wrinkled potatoes wait by the door to be planted.

"I'd like to know just what the hell it is you do in this house all day," he says, eyeing her up in the same way he sizes up a hog about to be slaughtered. Clara is still in her faded old bathrobe although it's nearly lunch time; she's forgotten to run a comb through her hair. She reaches up to tuck a limp strand behind her ear then pours a cup of coffee, the fresh brew just barely masking the stench of the slop pail under the sink.

Earl stares her down, and Clara knows he's itching to pick a fight like he usually does when something's gone wrong on the farm. "Blew the water pump on the tractor, in case you're interested," he finally says. "Going to take a couple days to get parts."

"A couple days? We can't afford to lose a couple of days. I heard the Bilyks are nearly done seeding," Clara blurts out without thinking. She hates to engage him when he gets like this, but it's been weeks since the poplars have started to bud, and Earl, as usual, has just pulled the tractor out of the shed.

They've fallen behind on the land payment again and she's the one lying awake at night, losing sleep over it. Another early frost in September and they'll be finished. The bank will foreclose. They'll lose the home quarter, this old house that belonged to his parents, and she and Jolene will have nowhere to go. Just because she let Earl talk her into signing some damn paper.

He lights up a smoke, casually, like he has all the time in the world. "If I could afford a second tractor and a hired man like the Bilyks, maybe I'd be done, too."

Earl isn't cut out for farming. He'd said so himself, shortly after they met in the lunchroom at the Ford Motor Company, where they both worked. He had stopped in Ontario on his way home to the prairies after the war, planning to stay for a year. Eventually, that year stretched closer to ten and he was still there when Clara was hired.

It was her first job; she filed papers, delivered mail, and made coffee in the main office. Much older than the boys Clara was used to dating, Earl was something to look at, with that swoop of black hair falling across his forehead and a cigarette always dangling from his lip. He was charming to a fault, and persuasive. His friend Chuck used to say Earl could sell foam off the ocean.

"When you gonna go out with me, hey, Miss Clara McDougall?"

"I'll never go out with you, Earl," Clara teased back. "My mama says I shouldn't date any man ten years older than me. She says you'll expire by the time I'm fifty, shrivel right up to nothing, and what'll I do without a functioning man while I'm still young?"

"I ain't never gonna be less of a man than the one you see standing here in front of you right now." His sleeves were rolled up and he flexed his bulging muscles, grinning at her with that toothy smile. "C'mon, pretty thing, don't make me beg."

Eventually, he wore her down and she slept with him at the rooming house where he stayed. He was the first man she'd ever been with and he taught her things; things that would make her blush in the light of day when she thought about them. He was ravenous, demanding, and she couldn't get her fill of him, either.

Three months later, she was pregnant. Twirling her in his arms, he kissed her with those hungry lips and promised her the world. After a quick wedding, he took her home to Manitoba on the train. His mother and father, in their eighties by now, had been waiting for their only son to come home and take over the farm. They retired to a small house in town and Clara and Earl moved into the farmhouse.

"Maybe you ought to get them potatoes planted," Earl says, breathing out a last curl of smoke as he pushes away from the table. "I hear Sarah Bilyk's potatoes are already up. I'll be back for lunch and you better have a hot meal on the table for a change."

The afternoon is almost gone. Clara sighs and pours herself another cup of coffee. She finally got dressed and brushed her stubborn hair, but she can't muster up the energy to lug the potatoes out to the garden. She'll wait until Jolene is home from school and they'll plant them together. It's too early to start thinking about supper so she pulls her box out of the oven and puts it on the table. She's keen to finish the sketch she was working on this morning. Just as she takes the lid off the box, there's a soft tap at the door.

"Ding dong. Avon calling." It's Joan Wright, the banker's wife, waving a small white bag. She lives in town in a new brick house along the river and sells beauty products for something to do while her boys are in school. Stylish and slender, she reminds Clara of the women who worked behind the gleaming glass counters at the Hudson's Bay, selling perfume and cosmetics, when she was a girl.

Today Joan's wearing a sleeveless summer shift, even though it's still a little cool out. The dress has a matching narrow belt in the same peachy floral fabric, with a small gold clasp the size of a silver dollar centred on her waist. She's draped an ecru coloured cardigan over her shoulders, reminding Clara of a photo she once saw of Jackie Kennedy Onassis.

Clara looks forward to Joan's monthly visit when the order comes in. She doesn't get many visitors, except old Mrs. Poole who comes by once a week to buy eggs. Earl won't let her drive the truck, and when he takes her to town on Saturday afternoons, she's more likely to go to the matinee with Jolene than sit at the Rex café listening to the gossip of other farm wives. It's a contest, she's learned, each woman trying to outdo the other. Bragging about their kids and their gardens. Who had the longest labour. Who dilled the most cucumbers and put up the most jars of raspberry jam. Who cares? Clara finds she has nothing to say. Amid the chatter, Clara realizes she's never fit in. The women all are connected in some way. One is married to someone else's first cousin, or their mothers went to school together, and it's lonely, being the outsider.

That's why she likes Joan. She's from somewhere else, too, and Clara enjoys hearing her stories. Joan has told her about all the different towns she's lived in as they follow her husband's job all over the province. She talks about her boys. They're always on the go. One of them is a star pitcher in his baseball league so they travel around during the summer, and haul the other one around all winter for hockey.

Jolene can't take part in any sports, not even volleyball where the kids ride a school bus to games. Earl won't allow it. He won't let Clara take the truck to town to pick Jolene up after practice, saying there's no money for gas. But Clara knows he just doesn't want her to go into town on her own.

Joan gets her hair done at Cuts and Curls Beauty Salon once a week. Clara never goes to the hairdresser—she cuts Jolene's and her own hair—although she washed and set her hair in rollers and Jenny gave her a comb out that one time when Earl's niece got married. It was nice, sitting in the pump-up chair, acting like a lady with more than two dollars in her purse. Joan told her they often take the boys for ice-cream to the Dairi-Dipp in Locklin. Earl would have a stroke if she asked him to drive twenty miles for anything else but the dentist.

Sometimes Clara wishes she could try on Joan's life for herself. Just slip into it like she was borrowing one of her pencil skirts, or a pair of her high-heeled shoes.

Every month Clara buys something from the catalogue: lotion, or a new lipstick, and once, a bottle of aftershave for Earl (that he never uses). The first time Joan came by, she made up Clara's face. Foundation and creamy violet eyeshadow. Three coats of mascara.

"My word," Joan had said, holding Clara's thick, dark hair away from her face. "Who knew you were this beautiful?"

Clara looked at herself in the mirror. She wouldn't call herself even half-assed pretty, let alone beautiful. All she could see was a washed-out woman, worn down by time and worry and Earl.

"I've got a new lipstick I think you'll love," Joan says, opening up a little turquoise box filled with sample tubes the size of Jolene's baby finger. Clara takes it and draws a tiny red crescent on her wrist.

"Oh, for heaven's sake," Joan says, holding out a small round mirror. "Try it on. Hold your lips like I showed you."

It's pretty, the colour of winter cranberries, but Clara doesn't need any more lipstick. She has a collection of over a dozen tubes hidden in her underwear drawer. And the egg money she's set aside this month is meant to buy a new spring jacket for Jolene, but she has to pick something to make sure Joan will keep stopping by.

"It's on sale this month," Joan adds. "A special promotion that's not in the book." There always seems to be a discount on whatever Clara chooses, making her wonder if Joan knows about their money troubles. Her husband, David, seems like the kind of man who might confide in his wife, and Joan is the sort of wife who would keep a secret like that.

Earl's land payment is overdue, and right after lunch, David called from the bank, asking to speak to him. Clara pictured him behind his desk, hand smooth as a hen's egg, cradling the phone to his ear.

"I'm sorry but Earl's just left."

"I suppose you know what this is about," he said in a voice so gentle it almost brought tears to her eyes.

He'd spoken to her in much the same way when she and Earl had gone to the bank last spring to sign papers. All the land was registered in Earl's name and she usually had no need to go to the bank with him when he borrowed more money. But that day, Earl told her to get dressed, they were going to town to see the banker.

"You understand you're giving up your dower rights under the Homestead Act. Even if your name's not on the title, the family home is protected under the law, and you must consent in writing before it can be mortgaged," David explained, coming out from behind his desk and pulling out her chair. He was a handsome man, as refined as Earl was crude, with a smooth-shaven face and understanding grey eyes.

Clara had never heard of the Homestead Act and she told David so.

"Just give her them papers to sign," Earl growled, massaging one hand against his grimy jeans. Clara had asked him to change before they went to town, at least put on a clean shirt, but Earl muttered under his breath and told her to get the hell in the truck.

"I can't have her sign this until she's received adequate counsel. You need to take this across the street to Irwin James and have him explain it to her."

"She don't need a lawyer to explain bugger all," Earl said, whacking his hand against the top of David's desk.

David picked up the phone. "I'm calling over. It'll only take a few minutes. Clara must understand the implications of waiving her rights."

"Waste of our damn time," Earl mumbled.

"It's the law, Earl. I have to do this. And Clara, you are not obligated to sign. You don't have to do this."

"Obligated, my ass," Earl said after they left. "You're obligated to do as I say, that's what." He twisted Clara's arm and told her no matter what Irwin James or the banker had to say, she was going to sign the god-damn paper.

While Clara pours tea into her best china cups, Joan packs up her beauty kit. Clara glances at the clock. There's still half an hour before Jolene will come home on the bus.

"What's this?" Joan has noticed Clara's box pushed to the side of the table. Before

Clara can react, Joan pulls out the drawings and fans them across the table like a winning hand of cards.

"Oh, it's Jolene! How old is she here?" Joan plucks out a sheet. "And this is Ida Piper, from the grocery store."

Clara's heart trips in her chest. "Oh, these silly drawings?" Before Joan can see any more, she sweeps her arms over the table, scoops up the sketches, and shoves them back in the box. A bright, burning flame spreads under her skin and she turns quickly away, fingers fumbling with a Tupperware container as she pulls out some cookies to put on a plate.

She can't let Joan see how flustered she is. How rattled.

This morning, while Clara was working on the sketch, she imagined soaking in the scent of David's woodsy cologne while her fingers lingered on his face, each pencil stroke a gentle caress. She bent her head to the paper and imagined tasting the sweetness of his tender lips. Even after dozens of drawings, she has yet to perfect each crease and every pore. His chiseled jaw, the strong angles of his bones.

She doesn't want Joan to know she borrows her husband's face. At night, she sees him when she closes her eyes. His whispery voice in her mind. "Clara, you don't have to do this." Drowning out the groans and making bearable the thrusting and grunting and the whiskers rasping against her skin.

Wills herself to believe it's him and not Earl.

CLARENCE MERLE KLYNE

Tan'si
What have I accomplished?

1 Life with my wife, Patsy, who is my first reader and best critic (calls it as she sees it).

2 Career as an English educator of more than thirty years which I enjoyed in its entirety.

3 Passion for reading and writing, from the time I picked up my first novel, discovering a passage into the world of story.

I self published my first two novels *The Silent March* (shortlisted for the Carol Shields award) and *The Gratitude of Wasps*. Both cover important Manitoba history when labour unions fought for the right to exist and to represent working people.

When Manitoba Theatre Projects (Chautauqua) toured the Interlake, prepandemic, I met some amazing, talented artists. This culminated in work with Claire Therese Friesen leading to my abridged story, *Don't Abuse the Dormouse*, being included in her film *I Carry Your Heart*.

Covid 19 isolation allowed me to write three more books for which I am seeking publishing partners. As a Métis writer I am proud of *Betula*, which tells the story of two Métis brothers who have very different life experiences.

Oh. #4! I am honoured profoundly, to have children, grandchildren and great grandchildren.

Maarsii

* *Photo by Patsy Klyne*

The Legend of Magpie: An Original Métis Story

Clarence Merle Klyne

When Peter Pangman dit Grivois fell in love he was on the wrong side of the water. This had been his story forever. On his first buffalo hunt at fourteen he recalled how, one evening, the hunting party packed the canoes and crossed the Souris River. Next morning they stood, astonished at the sight of thousands of buffalo grazing upon the very spot they'd left the night before.

Then came the terrible shame of losing the horses. Sixteen of his father's prime animals to be delivered to the RCMP depot. He'd forced the herd into the water and managed all but two across safely. He went back to retrieve the balky protesters but had to chase them about and get a rope on one so the other would follow. He'd wasted at least an hour, and just when he was about to lead them into the river, he looked up to see the main herd being rounded up and driven off. He sat upon his horse on the wrong side, helpless to do anything except watch. They were never recovered. His father muttered, groused, and cursed for months.

There had been other incidents. Too many of them. Always the water between him and his destiny. But this was the worst.

He gazed across the Lake Manitoba narrows. He thought of her, Marie Carriere. Hair black as a raven's back and soft to touch. Hesitant and shy. So charming. Ambling with grace. Loving and caring.

Embarrassed, he realized he was standing with a foolish grin spread across his face. His eyes darted about but of course there was no one else around. Their idea of a joke. To push off and paddle to the other side and leave him. They knew he was in love. That's why they'd left him. Laughing at his mooning about. Worse, knowing he was a hopeless swimmer, his friends used his weakness to abandon him.

His eyes fell upon a magpie who was scrounging the ground for insects. When the bird greeted him with a laugh and said, "Taanishi," Peter stepped back in surprise.

Automatically he raised his hat and tipped it. He remembered his Grandfather and smiled. To Peter, his Mooshoom had always been special. Hours spent together. Amazing tales and stories. Sharing language, family history, strange events. Hunting and trapping. Tragedy and comedy. A life lived.

And he remembered learning and his Grandfather saying "kisakihitin" and ruffling his hair and laughing. In the high hills

Mooshoom pointed out a moose with a young one.

Peter whispered, "There's a bird on its back."

"Yes. La keu di renn. He helps the moose. See." Mooshoom pointed, "He picks the ticks off. He will stay and clean him, and the moose will be strong and not get sick."

"But I thought they were only pests. They steal and make noise and cause trouble, Mooshoom."

"Yes. I've heard that before about them."

"Some of the kids shoot at them."

"Well," Mooshoom grinned, "I suppose we better hope they don't shoot back."

Peter laughed. "Ha! La keu di renn can't shoot, Grandfather."

"When I was your age, maybe a bit older, I hunted for the first time with my father. Not the buffalo. I was too young then. Geese. But I shot everything that day. Squirrels. A skunk. Crows. And, like your friends, I shot a magpie. Later I wished I hadn't."

"Why, Mooshoom?"

"It made my father angry and he took my gun. He said I was too young. *Now who's going to clean up after everything? Will it be you?* And that night I had a dream. Very strange. I was walking in the high grass, sneaking up on the deer. Careful not to make a sound. It took a long time to get close enough to shoot. Just as I raised my gun a magpie flew in front of me and started that awful laugh they make. Then hundreds of them appeared in the sky making the worst sound you ever heard. Screeching, squawking, flapping about over my head. Suddenly, a great ocean appeared before me and the deer were too far away. Gone."

Peter was intrigued and leaned into the story, "What happened then?"

"I woke up."

"That's not a very good story, Mooshoom."

"No. It's not. When I told my father about the dream, he said they are shooting back. I didn't even know they could do that."

"What did you do? Did you kill them? The magpies?"

"No. That would have made it worse. I did the only thing I could.

When your father was born, I taught him to always tip your hat to the magpie, son and he will do you a good turn."

The talking magpie cocked an eye and appeared to nod at him. "Tanshii Gordo niiya."

"I'm Peter. How did you learn to speak?"

"Su manzhii?"

"Sorry. No. I've no food." "La galet?"

Peter grinned, "No. No bannock. Nothing."

"Ma mere fay la bon galet."

"I'm sure she made wonderful bannock." Peter snorted in derision. "What am I doing standing here talking to a damned magpie?"

Gordo raised his sleek head in a proud fashion and began to move away. Scorned, he resumed his food search along the shore. Peter Pangman studied him with more attention. He tried to recall more of Mooshoom's teachings.

Peter had been told some people hated Magpie and even thought him an associate of Satan. Others claimed it depended on how many you saw together. Four meant death. Or was it birth? Perhaps both. Mooshoom said Magpie was spiritual and that was obvious since he was so like a human.

"A human? What do you mean?" Peter asked.

Mooshoom grinned, "Well. Just listen to one. He will chatter and cackle like a crone. Whistle to call up a mate. Warble like a braggart and even bark like a dog. And, just like people, he'll steal from you if he gets the chance."

Gordo darted forward and snapped up a beetle which he devoured. "Listen, Gordo. I did not mean to insult you or to despise your company. The fact is I'm supposed to be across the water …." Peter pointed to emphasize. "Tonight I'm supposed to meet Marie Carriere, the most beautiful creature who …." He was about to extrapolate upon this extraordinary woman but dropped his arm to his side. Forlorn and despondent.

Gordo ventured closer. “I can help you but if I do you must help me.”

“Huh. How can you help? You’re just a bird.”

Again the magpie drew himself to full height and began to move away. He glared at Peter, “We corvids have been maligned through history. My ancestors were abused, exploited, and falsely accused. Your own troubles seem trifling. Perhaps I should not bother helping you.”

“Okay. Alright.” Peter hastened, “My, but you get offended very easily.”

Gordo switched his tail and flapped his wings. He bristled, “You might too if you were even a little empathic. We Magpies have been denigrated to an absurdity! Vilified! Denounced! Even hunted!”

Peter opened his mouth, “You have quite a vocabulary. I am sure everything you’ve said is true.”

Gordo squinted a shining eye at Peter Pangman, as if measuring his sincerity. “Still, I will help you.”

“Thank you. I just don’t see how you can.”

“I will carry a message. You tell me what to say and I will fly to Marie Carriere and carry your love in my heart and in my throat. But in return, you must help me gather food now and later. And I will pursue her on your behalf.”

Peter thought, then affirmed, “Alright. What do you eat?”

“Many things. Bugs, worms, seeds. Even mice. Be industrious and you will be repaid many times over. I’m fond of blood-filled ticks so if you find a moose and pick some off it would be delicious. I would shout your virtues to Carriere for such a treat.”

Peter reached into his pocket, “And will you give her my gift of this shiny necklace?”

Gordo was struck by the brilliance of the stones. He eyed their loveliness and in his heart he coveted the treasure. Blues, greens and reds rained upon his eye until he was mesmerized. He forced himself to look away to hide his greed. He dared not look again but said “Of course. It is my duty to bestow gifts upon friends”.

For hours they scampered about for food while Gordo committed to memory all the love syllables Peter could create. Bugs, flies, and spiders were consumed in a monstrous banquet of indulgence. At one point Peter gazed at the constant gluttony of his companion and thought, *if you do not stop eating you won’t be able to fly*.

Finally, as it grew dark, Gordo, his belly distended and smacking his beak took wing and wobbled gracelessly into the air. He flew over Peter’s head twice and instructed him, “Remember to gather food for me. And find a moose with ticks. They are quite delicious, you know. You might try some for yourself, Peter. I know you are disgusted by my diet but there is an old saying among corvids. Never mock another's choices if your own cannot stand up to scrutiny.

So, if you find ticks today, eat them. Tomorrow they will be gone. Find them for me and I will make your dreams come true and you will bless us scavengers ever after."

He swooped and dropped a great blob of excrement on a rock at Peter's feet before he pointed his beak toward the west side of Lake Manitoba. Truthfully, it was a struggle to fly with a belly so full, his thoughts consumed by the gorgeous shiny necklace he carried hidden from the eyes of others. It took him a long time, and the sun had dropped and the moon had risen before he reached land.

Soon enough he discovered Marie Carriere sitting in a clearing by the water. The full moon glowed upon her beauty. Her long black locks glistened and reflected glorious shafts of light. Magpie thought that it was true; she was an exquisite female human. Why she may even be able to lift above the earth and float, so light and buoyant she seemed in her grace.

Gordo alighted close by.

He cleared his throat and in his raspy voice said, "Your beauty exceeds the blooms of the flowers."

She sat up straight, immediately on guard. Rising slowly, she gazed about in the moonlight. Did someone speak? Had she really heard a voice?

Magpie waited for a response. Finally, he croaked, "Sweet. Like clover when the bees are upon it."

A strange sound she thought. She was not afraid, only curious. "Show yourself. Your words are like Peter's but your voice is like brambles." Gordo cocked his head. He flapped into the air and alighted on a large rock closer to her. He thought about what to say.

"And yours is a songbird that spreads joy and goodness."

She stared at him and crept to the rock. Her eyes widened as Magpie puffed himself up and whistled. He flapped and bobbed his head. "The earth that you walk upon feels itself blessed."

Her hands flew to her cheeks as she stood enraptured. She wavered between nervous tension and a slight giddiness in the stomach. Fascination with the creature finally prevailed.

"I have been told that those such as you speak, but I never thought to hear it. And where did you learn to be so sweet?"

"Ki shaakiihitin salay."

She was astounded. "Why! That's what Peter calls me. But you could not know that!! Unless…." The thought seemed so bizarre that she almost did not utter it.

"Are you a shapeshifter, Peter? Have you changed yourself? Mother told me of such things, but I never thought to see it. The boys laughed when they returned in the canoes without you, but I did not think it funny. Ha! What would they say now if they could see you with that long, proud tail and those beautifully coloured feathers. So long as you don't speak, you are quite attractive and my hands long to touch your breast and stroke your neck."

Gordo began to clean his wings with his long beak. He preened and strutted upon the rock. The moon's light caressed his grand shapeliness as he did a polished twirl and leap. He shouted and warbled a dreadful crackling musical note that caused Marie's ear to rebel.

"Oh, please stop," she pleaded. "Let me, Peter."

When she stood and opened her mouth the sweet lilting uttering caused the air to shimmer in ecstasy. Across the water Peter Pangman dit Grivois heard the enticing siren strains, and, maddened with desire, he stomped up and down the beach. He pulled at his hair and tore his clothing from his body. Mindlessly he rushed toward the sound and was very wet before he remembered that he could not swim.

Gordo called out, "Let us dance to the music of love."

And they did. She moved toward him, and her willowy body waved, shimmered, and flowed in the moon's silver light. Gordo stretched and posed, whistled, and whispered and whirled about.

He took flight and as she danced he swooped around her. Wingtips touched her face, torso, and legs. Flutters, caresses, tremulations. Her whole world became the dance. So entrenched in it she was unaware when her body faded and returned and then lapsed into an ethereal shadow. She neither saw nor felt when the magpie reached deep into his tail feathers and grasped the necklace. He flung it skyward and it floated above Marie, then settled softly about her neck and rested.

The dance continued 'til dawn. When the sun began its daily struggle to emerge, Gordo said, "Come my love. It is time." He and the beautiful female took to the air and flew east.

Peter awoke very early. He sat up, startled that he'd slept the night away. He retrieved his clothes and dressed himself and groused that Gordo had failed to return. But he recalled Mooshoom's advice, so he gathered a plentiful supply of food for Gordo while his own stomach growled with need. Why had the magpie not returned with a message from his lover? He gazed across the water and thought he saw two birds approaching.

When they reached him, he watched for them to land, waved at them when they circled once and then a second time. Now the sun was peeking over the trees and while Peter stood in the shade of an embankment the sun shone on the flying figures. He could see a glint and reflection on one of the flyers. A startling, piercing array of colours streamed from the sky and framed him momentarily.

The figures rode the air currents with an easy flow of curving arcs. One of them leaned into the other until their wingtips touched and wavered in the early morning light. Then they turned as one and directed their flight back toward the west.

Peter sighed. Oh, how he hated always being on the wrong side of the water.

SHARON MCINNES

Sharon McInnes is the author of *Across a Narrow Strait*, a novel, and *Up Close & Personal: Confessions of a Backyard Birder*. Her articles have appeared in magazines, professional journals, and newspapers. In 2012, her essay, "Formative Years," was included in *Writing the West Coast: Artful Identities*. In 2019, she began writing short stories. In 2020, "The David and Goliath" was published in *Island Writer Magazine*, "A Symphony of Sparrows" took second prize for fiction in Askew's Word on the Lake Contest, and "Various Functions of Fire" took first place for fiction in the Victoria Writers Society Contest. Also, "The Neighbour" was shortlisted for the Federation of BC Writers BC & Yukon Short Fiction Contest, then won second prize for fiction in the Melody Richardson Memorial Contest. Sharon recently finished a memoir about the profound impact of her mother's diagnosis of vascular dementia on her and on their mother-daughter relationship. Two essays based on that material have been published - "Disappearing" in *Island Writer Magazine* and "Like Morning Glory Vines" at Grief Dialogues. Sharon lives in Cumberland, BC, where she loves spending time hanging out with her adorable three-year-old grandson.

** Photo by Brie McInnes*

The Redhead

Sharon McInnes

Stopped at a red light, Harold is griping to himself about the damn bird when a black SUV shoots past on the right and a green Miata convertible enters the intersection from the left. He blasts the horn. The Miata swerves, spins, comes to a halt. There is no collision. A small plane does not hit a mountain. Drivers of two other cars run toward the Miata. Harold pulls his dark blue Jetta over, parks in front of a café, sits waiting for his limbic system to calm, waiting for the images in his head to clear. Not images of the SUV and the convertible; images of the small plane and the mountain. Not that he'd seen that collision. He'd been mowing the lawn at the time. But his mind held multiple versions of the event, imagined versions, versions that had woken him in the night in a cold sweat for the past six weeks.

The café is crowded. He sits on a stool by the window and sips on a steaming black coffee. He should be in the classroom. Today's lesson is on the Pythagorean theorem. *In a right angle triangle, the square of the hypotenuse is equal to the sum of the squares of the other two sides.* Always. Harold finds Pythagoras comforting. Rose had been comforting, too.

The last time he saw Rose, the last time he would ever again see her, they'd been at the breakfast table, her with her country-style granola and almond milk, him with his bacon and eggs-over-easy. The scent of freshly brewed coffee had filled the kitchen. They were eating in what he would now call companionable silence until she said, "I'd really like you to finish the cottage this summer, hon."

Not this again. "Yeah, I'll try." Same answer he'd been giving her for three and a half years.

"I'd love for the kids to come for Thanksgiving."

"I know you would." Don't you have to get to the airport?

Rose had sighed. "Harry, please. It's time." "I will, I will." *Will I?*

"Do you promise?"

"I do." As he said those loaded words, Carmen, their neighbour, poked her head in the front door. "Ready to go, Rose?"

"Ready!" She took one last gulp of coffee, hugged Harold good-bye, picked up her suitcase, and was gone. Had he told her that he loved her? Because he did. Does.

The day the plane hit the mountain, the once-perfectly-tilted axis of Harold's world slipped, leaving everything slightly askew, off-balance. This made decision-making almost impossible. What to eat for dinner? What show to watch? How many glasses of scotch to down? He had no idea. It was as if life was happening *to* him, as if he'd lost all agency, direction, control. Oh, he managed to get to work, to spend the day teaching five classes of geometry and algebra, and to drive home again. But once he got in the door he collapsed onto the sofa and stared into space until his stomach, an hour or two later, insisted he at least have a peanut butter sandwich. How long could a man live on PB sandwiches? And now, to make matters worse, he was being harassed. By a bloody red-headed sapsucker. For the last week, it had been drumming on the metal chimney pipe on his roof every day at dawn. The first time it happened, he thought the house was about to explode. Maybe that wouldn't have been so bad.

They'd bought the house, a nine-hundred-square-foot bungalow with one bedroom, one bathroom, a spacious living room with a real fireplace and vaulted ceilings, four years ago. It was his idea. He didn't want to wait until retirement to spend his evenings on a deck overlooking a lake. Was that too much to ask? Rose had succumbed, with one stipulation. *Build a cottage so the kids can come and stay.*

He laid the foundation and did the framing that first summer. Somehow, though, over the next three years, he never found the time or energy to go any further. It had no insulation, no plumbing, no electricity, no siding. Wouldn't it be better if the kids, especially his know-it-all son-in-law, Bradley, stayed in a motel in town? Rose had disagreed, strongly. They had seen things differently.

When you thought about it, they'd seen a lot of things differently, led quite separate lives. Rose had gone to Mexico with girlfriends every winter. Harold hated travelling. Rose had belonged to a monthly book club. Harold avoided groups, stayed home, did the NYT crossword. She'd traipsed around the island with Carmen on her quest for second-hand furniture. Harold still stayed home.

The only thing he and Rose had done as a couple was watch birds. She'd become interested in the delicate little creatures when they moved to the lake. And seeing them flit around and fight for their territory, his curiosity had been piqued, too. He'd built a few platform feeders, installed a gravity-fed pond, and fed the hummingbirds when Rose was out of town. Last spring they'd watched a pair of red-headed sapsuckers build their nest in the broadleaf maple in the front yard. Once the eggs were laid, they spent endless hours observing the nest. Those parents were vigilant. They took turns sitting on the eggs, brought food back and forth to each other, and constantly scanned the sky for predators. After the chicks hatched, things got even busier, what with all the cheeping for food, and the need to pick bugs out of the babies' feathers, and the increased predator control because of the noise those fragile wee things made. It went on for twenty-seven days. When they finally fledged, leaping out of the tree into thin air, Rose had clapped and cheered as if her first born had won the Nobel Prize. A bit over the top. He'd say this, though: she'd taught him a lot about birds. Like the fact that a woodpecker's undulating flight pattern required less energy than a steady flight pattern. Birds were masters of efficiency, an admirable trait, even if it was all in the service of survival. He appreciated that.

The cops are on the scene. It looks like everyone is okay. His hands are still clammy, his heart still pounding. In twenty-one years of teaching, he has never been late until this last six weeks. If you count today—a foregone conclusion—he will have been late three times since Rose died. *Will have been late*: the future perfect, a rarely used tense. Because, really, it assumes so much. We all assume so much, though, don't we? Harold had assumed that while Rose was at her sister's, he would enjoy a week of freedom. Freedom from what? It's not that anyone was forcing him to do anything. What was he hoping to escape?

The plane was a small Cessna. It had hit a mountain outside Lytton. Crash investigators said there was no fog and no evidence of mechanical failure. It must have been pilot error. He died too. They all did. He takes a final sip of coffee, gets back in the car, drives to school, remembers.

One hundred and fifty people had shown up for the funeral. Harold had recognized a handful, maybe twenty. The unknowns were Rose's colleagues and family members of her patients. Many came forward to say a few words. They talked about her warmth and kindness and sense of humour. She wasn't one of those managers who sat in their office pushing numbers around; she was out there assisting the residents, helping them get dressed, walking them to the dining room, encouraging them to try a new activity. It made him proud. Had she known he was proud of her?

It was Harold's habit—once *their* habit—to sit on the back deck drinking his morning coffee. Now the damn bird joins him. He'll no sooner settle in with his coffee and the paper than it flies over, lands on the pergola beside the deck, and stares, even glares. *What is it that you want, exactly?* The bird is persistent. *Are you trying to get me to go inside? Because I am not doing that. I like it out here.* He'll give his newspaper a shake and bury his head in its pages. The bird will start drumming then, like a toddler acting up when his Mommy's on the phone.

The day before the car accident Carmen had surprised Harold by showing up at lunchtime with two roast beef sandwiches made with real roast beef and horseradish and two bottles of home-made cider. At first, he didn't know what to make of it. Now that Rose was gone, did Carmen plan to reveal a long-held crush on him, the older man next door? But no. As he took a bite, she'd looked him in the eye, her brow creased, and said, in an extremely irritating voice, "How are you doing, Harry?" *Dooo-ing.* She stretched out the vowel.

He chewed, swallowed. "Dooo-ing?"

"Yes. Doing. … Emotionally."

Emotionally? "Fine. I'm doing fine." Emotionally.

"Are you?" She continued to peer into his eyes, her forehead wrinkling even more, like an accordion compressing.

"I am." He looked her straight in the eye too, like a man who wasn't in the least bit afraid of where this conversation was heading.

She backed off then, looked away, scanned the kitchen, her head shaking, sadly. Two months ago, the kitchen, with its central island and deep double sinks and gleaming stainless steel pots and pans, would have been, in Rose's words, spic and span. Today the counters were piled high with empty take-out cartons, the pans were definitely not gleaming, and there was an unpleasant odour in the room.

Fear turned to irritation. “Why do you ask, Carmen? Does it look like I’m falling apart or something?”

Her brows arched, her head tilting to the left, she said, “Well, maybe.”

Maybe? Of course, I’m falling part. Floodgates straining, he stood up. “I have to use the washroom. Excuse me.”

The medicine cabinet was mirrored. He opened it, slipped one of the tiny green pills the doctor had given him—to be used only in an emergency—under his tongue, closed his eyes, and took four deep breaths. *One final breath, let it all go.* Opening his eyes, he closed the door of the cabinet and looked in the mirror. The man he saw was tall and thin with a beard, a fast-receding hairline, and dark-rimmed glasses. Sadness clung to him like lint. He took his glasses off, stared at a fuzzy version of himself. Out of the blur, a memory.

He’d been watching a TV movie. The main character, played by a stoic William Hurt, reminded him of his father. As the character slammed a door, Harold had, inexplicably, broken down, sobbing uncontrollably, like a kid standing at the end of the driveway watching his family drive away, forever. Before he knew it, snot was running into his carefully trimmed beard.

It wasn't that his father was abusive. He was simply … reserved. Possibly antisocial. They never had people over. Harry's friends were not allowed to visit unless they stayed in his room and played quietly. Luckily, Harold's Mom had been normal. If only she'd lived past his thirteenth birthday. Little Harry had decided early not to follow in his father's footsteps, to create his own path. That's probably why he'd been attracted to Rose. She wasn't a conventionally pretty woman—she had a prominent nose, always carried an extra twenty pounds, and her wavy red hair wasn't his preferred style—but she was a happy, affectionate extrovert, and after spending one evening with her at his cousin's wedding, he'd known she was the one. Thirty years later, watching that TV movie, he'd seen it for the first time: he'd charged her with stopping him from becoming his father.

Carmen had still been there when he returned to the kitchen. Arms crossed, forehead furrowed, she'd said, "Harry, I just want to say this and then I'll shut up. You should go talk to someone." She handed him a card. "Jack saw this guy for a while after his dad died."

Talk to a stranger? "Thanks, Carmen."

That evening he'd sat at his office desk eating a take-out burger and staring at the poster above his head. Rose had bought it for him. *There is geometry in the humming of the strings, there is music in the spacing of the spheres.* Some of Pythagorus's later ideas flirted with what certain academics considered to verge on the realm of magic. If Rose had understood it, she'd have bought it, hook, line, and sinker. Just like she believed in her Tarot cards. Carmen said she had a gift for it. She read for friends and at parties, and even, apparently, for some of the residents at the care home, if she thought it would ease their suffering. Did she know that plane would crash?

Hauling himself out of his chair, he'd poured another coffee, opened the sliding door, and immediately wished he hadn't. There it stood, on the bluff, a bare-boned skeleton. He could almost hear her voice. *Sure like to see the cottage finished ... blab bla bla.* The bird had flown into his view then, landing in the cedar tree. *Oh, you again.* It leapt into midair and flew toward him, landing on the post beside the deck. *What do you want with me? I don't have a cache of bugs in my back pocket, you know.* Its head jerked up and down, as if nodding. Harold looked into its black eyes. He'd never been so close to a bird. Bright red head. White spot in front of the eye. Beige stripe above the sharp bill. A chill ran up his spine. *Just go away, will you? Leave me in peace!* Harold turned around, closed the door, plopped into his Lazy Boy. The bird had remained on the post, watching.

On the evening of the last day of school for the year, Harold pours himself a double scotch. What will he do all summer? The two months of free time stretching out before him feel ... dangerous. He imagines tectonic plates shifting, the shaking of the earth, the rolling waves of a tsunami.

The back door opens. "Happy birthday, Harry." Carmen places a package in his hands.

Oh God. Today's my birthday.

"What's this?" She'd never bought him a birthday present before.

"It's from Rose. She hid it at our place so you wouldn't find it."

He stares at the package for several seconds before pulling off the yellow ribbons and bright blue wrapping paper. A book. *Pythagoras: The Man and His World.* How had he missed this one? He scans the table of contents. *Numerology. Asceticism. The Transmigration of Souls ...*

As he fingers the book, an odd sensation overcomes him. Tingling in his fingers, tears backing up behind his eyes. And then the drumming starts, loud and insistent. He turns to look. There, on the cottage roof. He puts the book on the table and steps outside, without thinking, then down the two stairs onto the grass. The sapsucker turns its head in his direction. He stands in the middle of the lawn, motionless, still. It flies down into the cottage, lands on a two-by-four between rooms that, according to the plans, are the kitchen and bathroom, and tilts its head, almost coyly. He takes three slow steps toward it. Then two more steps. He is six feet away when it flies directly toward him, grabs the window frame, and blinks. He blinks too, blinks back tears, is overcome with a sensation of warmth, of something verging on happiness. *What's happening to me?*

That night he sleeps peacefully. And for the next week, he wakes at dawn to the drumming of the sapsucker. He leaps out of bed to peer out the window. It's there, in the maple, waiting. He pulls on his tartan bathrobe and the sheepskin slippers Rose bought him years ago and sits on the back deck with a cup of coffee and slice of whole-wheat toast and peanut butter. The bird joins him. The earth begins to spin, once again, on its perfectly tilted axis.

It's time.

For the next eight weeks, as he saws boards and hammers nails, as he installs counters and plumbing, as he builds the brick fireplace Rose had always wanted, the sapsucker is always close by. Sometimes, in the beginning, Harold teases it. *Don't you have something better to do? You think you're my supervisor or something?* Then, one day, as the bird sits on the window ledge watching him work, he finds himself apologizing. *I'm sorry. I'm sorry I was so damn stubborn. I'm sorry it's too late.* The bird blinks, tilts its head, nods.

*

The smell of roasting turkey fills the cottage. Carmen and Susan stand at the sink in aprons, peeling carrots, telling Rose stories, laughing. Jack and Bradley argue politics at the round oak table Carmen hunted down. The grandkids, Megan and Noah, teenagers now, sprawl in front of the fireplace, their noses in their devices. Harold stands in the doorway, watching. When Susan sees him, she hurries over and hugs him. It is their second hug of the day.

Jack is out of his chair and pouring wine for everyone. "Harry! Get in here, you old coot! Time for a toast." The adults gather. Jack hollers at Megan and Noah, "Kids! You too." He pours a soft drink for them and raises his glass. "To Rose. She'd be so happy to see everyone together in this beauty of a cottage."

Harold nods and lifts his glass. "She would." Then, out of the corner of his eye, he sees movement and hears the flap of wings. And there she is, gripping the fireplace bricks. His heart suddenly full, his eyes suddenly wet, he raises a glass of Pinot Gris to the lovely red-headed bird, and smiles. "To you, sweetheart." His family and friends look in the direction of the fireplace, their foreheads creased, then glance at one another, bewilderment written on their faces.

ELEONORE SCHÖNMAIER

Eleonore Schönmaier was born and raised in a northern Canadian wilderness settlement. Her newest poetry collection is *Field Guide to the Lost Flower of Crete* (McGill-Queen's University Press, 2021). *Wavelengths of Your Song* (MQUP) was published in German translation as *Wellenlängen deines Liedes* (parasitenpresse, 2020). *Dust Blown Side of the Journey* (MQUP) was a finalist for the Eyelands Book Awards 2020 (Greece). She's the winner of the Alfred G. Bailey Prize, the Earle Birney Prize, and the National Broadsheet Contest, among others. Her poetry has been widely anthologized in the United States and Canada including in *Best Canadian*

Poetry. Multiple international composers have set her writing to music including Michalis Paraskakis and Emily Doolittle. Her fiction has been published in *The New Quarterly*, *The Antigonish Review* and was featured in the Boreality issue of *Prairie Fire*. Her short story "Sidereal Time" was a Sheldon Currie Fiction Award winner (second place). She is at work on a collection of linked stories.

The Other Side of the Map

Eleonore Schönmaier

In my Megwaakwaang lakeshore rental cabin a white-throated sparrow started into song at three. By four o'clock the eastern sky hung out its pastel sheets and I was wide awake. I couldn't blame my alertness on one hour's worth of jet lag and tossed and turned in bed. At five the float planes started to take off with a roar as if the world's end was being launched. They were transport planes, the link to the no-roads far north: land of lakes and endless bush. It was all a long way from my home in Toronto.

It was my first work trip since Tor and I were married one month ago, my first wedding at age thirty-eight. Though I will be happy to see Tor at the end of this round of travels, I can't say I specifically miss him. I admire his quiet ways, his focus on his woodworking business, but I need large doses of intensity. Mostly I'm looking forward to the novelty of a new place.

I looked at the clock again: 5:45. Opening my suitcase I wondered why I had packed two dresses to bring to the bush. Usually, I'm more practical than this. Was marriage already making me fuzzy-headed? I pulled on jeans and a red T-shirt and started to walk along the shore to Kenda's Anishinabek Outfitters. The lake was flat-calm with a few small bungalows along the shore. Behind the buildings the dark-green forest hung close like a thick shawl around the shoulders of the small village. It all looked like a child's attempt at civilization, an impromptu Lego set in colours of grey, brown and beige. One of the bungalows I passed had a small sign next to the door: *Kiishik's Dental Office*.

I started to imagine what it would be like living here with everyone knowing everyone else's business and no escape from the sameness of each day. The light on the water would be blue-bright one day and grey-black the next. Franny or Jack or Sally would or would not walk to the only cafe in town. I could use a cup of coffee myself but that would have to wait.

At the rear of Kenda's small green building, I knocked on the screen door and entered. Her view was awesome, right down the length of the lake with most of the shore fringed in spruce trees, and I was glad I'd agreed to the editor's Megwaakwaang travel-story pitch.

Kenda was seated behind a computer screen staring at a spreadsheet. Handing me a mug of Labrador tea she said, "I know you called me about this interview weeks ago, but in reality now's a really bad time."

"Thanks," I said, wishing I could have said no to the muddy hot water which she said was brewed from a local plant. Kenda had short black hair and was wearing faded jeans, and a green T-shirt featuring a canoe as her business logo. She vibrated restless energy as she sat upright in the wooden chair in her office above the boathouse.

I sat down in the only other chair, and Kenda leaned forward and said, "I'll be up front, but I hope you won't print the negative side of what's happened. My partner had to go to Winnipeg since that's where the nearest hospital is. The leeches will make a good story for you, but the accident won't help me promote my business." She picked up a quartz paper weight, and set it on top of a pile of colourful brochures on her desk. "I'm worried about Theo, but he says he'll be OK."

Kenda told me how as a child she dangled her feet in a creek in spring, and after found her soles covered in black baby-leech specks. The adult *Macrobdella decora* with its black back and bright orange belly was, however, not attached to Theo's water refreshed feet but to his reattached fingertips. He'd been chopping wood for the evening campfire when a tourist asked if he could try. Theo held the piece of wood in place on top of the chopping block, but the tourist didn't wait until he removed his hand before swinging the ax.

*

Unable to resist a good story, I flew to Winnipeg to visit Theo. At the Megwaakwaang airport, miles out of town, there was no security. If you wanted to you could pack your guns in your suitcase. Kenda had given me a plastic container of blueberries to give Theo as a gift, and I kept this in my purse so that the berries wouldn't get all jumbled, but I carried no guns. The Bearskin Air plane shuddered so hard after take-off it felt like flight had just been invented the day before. From the air I saw many lakes: the boreal forest looked as if it was re-emerging after a great flood. The conversation around me focused on northern health costs: having to fly to the city for hospital lab tests with the government only paying part of the fare.

At the hospital, I found Theo in the TV lounge watching baseball. Face and arms well-tanned, he sat in his blue gown. He was more worried about his replacement at work than about his almost-lost two fingers: red-pink, stitched and puffy. Theo said he'd no problems with the leeches, he just couldn't stand waiting to heal.

"The nurses apply leeches every four hours and this keeps the swelling down while my veins grow."

"So much for modern science," I said.

"The doctor told me that leeches have thirty-four body parts and thirty-four little brains. It'll be something to entertain the tourists with. I won't be letting anyone volunteer to chop the campfire wood anytime soon especially not with my fingers still in the way. I was lucky I didn't lose my hand." When he stopped talking the skin at the top of his nose scrunched up in furrows. This gave him an intense worried look even though his voice sounded calm.

"Kenda really admires you," I said.

"Did she talk about the guy who's filling in for me? He used to work there before me."

"Are you worried that you'll lose your job?" I tried not to stare at his legs sticking out from under his gown.

"I own half the business. It was Kenda's idea," Theo said.

"Then there shouldn't be a problem." Kenda had told me Theo's parents ran the local junkyard, but weekends they'd taken him canoeing and his paddling skills were supposedly superb.

"The guy's her ex."

Theo obviously had worries about being replaced in the bedroom rather than in the office, though one loss would inevitably lead to the other.

*

Kenda was a lot calmer when I returned to Megwaakwaang and I also met Theo's worst fear: Yann. He hoisted the canoes onto his shoulders as though they were small toys and talked philosophy on the side, an unusual and highly appealing combination. Kenda was sitting at the picnic table next to the boathouse with the list of the day's tourists in front of her. She was watching Yann put the canoes into the water. I slid in next to her, and told her Theo seemed to be doing fine. He had started to eat the blueberries right away, and my last impression of him was the purple colour of his lips.

I asked Kenda if leeches were a problem when the tourists went swimming. “I admit we don’t warn them ahead of time," she said. "If one gets stuck to their toe Theo pulls it off and jokes that leech removal costs are free.”

Yann was wearing a sleeveless shirt and I could see the sweat building on his arms and his forehead as he lifted and lowered the canoes. He had such physicality it was hard to imagine him as a philosophy doctoral student. “And mosquitoes?” I asked, trying to focus. I would have preferred to have girl-talk with Kenda about Yann and Theo.

“At night the mosquitoes hum like a power-generator. You don’t hear it so much in town, but the full-volume is there in the background when you do a starlight paddle.”

I’d seen T-shirts showing enormous mosquitoes carrying off a person like prey. I’d bought Deet, rubbed it into my skin and watched it eat a hole in my Gortex jacket.

"Eco-bug is best," Kenda said.

“Does it work? I asked.

“Sure,” she said.

She was savvy in her marketing tools, natural all the way.

*

In the afternoon I drove my rental jeep down the road leading out of town to get a better sense of the area. I saw clear-cuts right to the road's edge and down to the banks of the creek signed *Half Way*. Halfway to where I wondered? The remaining black spruce and Jack pines grew densely: stunted trees that would almost bend over if climbed by a large child.

An old man was riding a bicycle, and that was the sum total of traffic.

A sign read *Craven Lake* and after driving past abandoned mine buildings I came to a cluster of aluminum-siding houses. There was a group of young children and wolf-like dogs running about on the gravel road. When I asked a boy of ten if there was a store he said, "No, there's nothing," and it seemed to be true.

"Where you from?" he said, standing in front of me in his *Killer* T-shirt.

"I live out of my suitcase," I said.

"No way," he said.

"My apartment's in Toronto," I said.

"That's where I want to go," the boy said.

I counted only twenty-three houses and none anywhere near the lake. Most of the adults were young. I asked the children about the old man on the bike.

“Mr. C,” they said, and pointed to his compact white house.

The boy said, “He has a crashed car in his garage.”

I walked past the house slowly with some of the children following me. In Mr. C's yard there was a vegetable garden: potatoes, peas, carrots, radishes, green beans and lettuce. It was the only garden I'd seen, and I was surprised that you could even grow food this far north.

On the edge of the houses beside the boarded-up school was a large flat field, the earth cracked open in dried-out fissures with not so much as a blade of grass in sight. The children told me they bused to Megwaakwaang for classes.

“Cyanide field,” the boy said.

“Slime field,” said another girl. “It’s our playground, but we’re not allowed there anymore.”

Mine tailings too toxic for play, I found out that evening in Megwaakwaang.

*

I stood in the entrance adjusting to the dim light of the Snake Pit, the local bar in the basement of the Walleye Inn. Most of the clientele had the haggard faces of people who spent their grocery money on booze. The brown-paneling walls were covered with the trophy heads of moose and black bear. I felt like I was in a graveyard of the dead and the nearly dead. I slid onto the stool next to the only person who seemed to exude vitality. The man introduced himself as a "pilot with no license."

"Do you fly?" I asked.

"I'm the best around," he said.

I didn't believe his "I know how to fly so why go to school for a piece of paper." I wondered how he'd lost his license. He told me he'd grown up in Craven Lake and as a child he'd always played on the polluted fields.

"Can't see why the kids don't play there anymore. It's not like I have twelve toes or two heads."

No, but he did have olive skin and a startling pair of green eyes. He asked why I was in town, and I said I was there to visit Kenda.

"I went to school with her mother, back when there still was a school in Craven Lake. She's not what you'd call normal."

"Oh?" I said.

"She went south and became a lawyer type, but she came back to town. If you're going to go to all that trouble you might as well stay away, don't you think?"

I nodded, and imagined that it would take a lot of drive to grow up in Craven Lake and then go to a southern university. Kenda in her determination mirrored this drive, though she had taken a different route. "Kenda didn't study did she?" I asked.

"Yup," he said, swiveling his stool so that our knees touched. “Something to do with biology, but like her mother she boomeranged right back home.”

"I've been talking to her about her business."

“Went out in one of her bathtubs, did you?” he said. “She’s no Indian,” he added. “She’s an apple, red on the outside and white on the inside."

*

The next morning when I asked about her influences, Kenda told me some more about her family. When she mentioned her Austrian born grandfather I knew immediately that he was Mr. C. She said everyone in the entire district knew him, that he was always out on his bike even when it was minus thirty below.

“Opa has six different bicycles in his garage. He’s never owned a car. There’s always crazy stories about him floating around. He and my Oma split up years ago. She felt he was too extreme in his environmentalism.”

Kenda asked if I wanted to eat some cereal. "From organic oats. I mix in the fruit myself."

I said a reluctant yes, poured on the soya milk and started chewing. Brown paper bags labeled *Kenda’s Northern Museli* lined an office shelf.

“My Opa picks the blueberries, and I dry them in a special oven Theo built for me,” she said.

Theo, as far as I could see, had no worries. She mentioned him in every second sentence. "Are you close to your grandparents?"

"Yes, they've always been supportive of my work. I was adopted and it hasn’t been easy, but I know my Opa and Oma do love me in their own way."

That explained the pilot’s crude apple comment, though I didn’t tell Kenda this. She’d heard it all before at any rate, I was sure. I shuddered to think about all the racism she must face. There was so much I needed to learn including courage for I had remained silent when the pilot spoke about Kenda. I wanted to ask her all sorts of questions, but my thoughts felt frozen. All I said was, "My son was raised by my parents."

"My grandmother didn't raise me, but she's always been there for me. My parents wanted me to go into law. They think this business is a risky idea. Do you ever see your son?"

"I visit Pedro in Halifax, but I'm more like an aunt to him. I had him when I was fourteen. Do you plan on having kids?"

"I'm pregnant so I guess the answer is yes. My parents think twenty-two is too young to have a child. They waited too long to have kids, and I don’t want to repeat their mistakes. I want to start offering family tours."

I admired her ambition, and didn't dare ask who the father was. I didn't tell her a rapist was the father of my first child. What would be the point? Not even my parents know this. I live my life on my own terms with my own choices.

I took a photograph of Kenda sitting in the stern of one of her canoes, looking confident as if she had grown up with a paddle in her hand. She had told me she wasn't actually a great canoeist, that Theo was the sporty one while she managed the business. Soon she'd have a crib next to her desk.

*

On the flight south I started typing up the article, and in our Toronto home on my large computer screen I showed Tor some of the photos. He pointed to Kenda’s desk, to a framed photo of Theo that I’d only briefly noticed. “You and this guy could be brother and sister,” he said. Tor and I on the other hand are opposites: his blond curls contrast my long black hair.

“It’s just a photo of a photo. You’re thinking about that photographer we read about—she puts strangers side by side, and makes them look like family.”

“Like her I’m starting to match people up,” Tor said. “You should have photographed the guy who said he’s an ex-pilot.”

“No ex,” I said. “I asked around and he still goes up each morning."

“By himself?”

“No, with clients. The locals trust him. He’s saved lives with his medevacs. Kenda said if she expands her business, and starts taking people further north, she’ll use him too. She said the story he tells about his non-license is pure fiction. It's a tall tale he tells strangers in bars.”

I stooped down under my desk to grab my carry-on bag, and when I reached inside for Kenda’s business brochures I felt something small and fuzzy. “Yuck,” I said, and Tor looked at me as I pulled out a dead deer mouse. “At least it’s not a wolf- pelt,” I said. “The pilot offered me one if I slept with him.”

Tor looked at me not knowing if I was serious and said, “You didn’t, did you?”

I wanted badly to tell him the truth, but just as the words were on the tip of my tongue I realized the truth was crueler than a lie. “Only a mouse, no wolf in this bag,” I said. “But maybe I’ll write I slept with a bush pilot.”

“Hopefully not,” said Tor flipping through one of the brochures.

I did have a photograph of the pilot, standing in front of a yellow two-seater plane. He'd taken me up in the air, and not charged me a cent: the shadow of the plane over fields of fireweed, the purple flowers sprouting from the blackened soil after a recent burn.

The pilot had landed the float plane on Cat Lake. From behind his seat he pulled out a cooler: smoked pickerel sandwiches and cold beer. I kissed him on the mouth and he said, “That’s not worth a wolf-pelt, but I’ll give you a rabbit foot for luck. Though there’s really no such thing as luck. It’s just a rabbit foot.”

As we sat picnicking on the granite shore I showed the pilot the paperback I was carrying in my purse, but he was only interested in the title: *Out Stealing Horses.* He grinned and said, "That's something I'd like to try, stealing horses, except Alberta's a long ways away."

"Trond, the main character, keeps saying 'I've been lucky' but his dad abandoned him at fifteen, and his wife died in a car crash." I didn't mention that Trond doesn't live in cowboy country.

"My dad buggered off too when I was a kid," the pilot said.

After that I didn't have the heart to keep talking on about luck. I would have sounded more than foolish if I'd told him Faustus is Latin for lucky. Who the fuck cares about Faustus? he'd have said. I also didn’t tell him he’s an awful racist, but since I was attracted to him am I really any better?

I opened the accordion fold of the travel brochure and said to Tor, “Do you believe in luck?”

“When things turn out right,” Tor said, “like you and me.”

"I sometimes think luck is the tall tale people tell after the hard things that have happened—"

"I met you," Tor said. "That's a good thing not a bad thing. Or did your pilot have a better idea?"

I clicked with my mouse until the pilot appeared.

"He went up in a winter storm years ago trying to medivac an injured man to the Winnipeg hospital. But he crash landed and the nurse on board died."

"Why doesn't that surprise me." Tor said. "Did he tell you that or someone else?"

"I went up with him."

"And you survived," Tor said biting his lower lip.

"He knows what he's doing."

"I'm sure he does. He looks all cocky."

"Life is different up north. People take risks trying to do the right thing."

I clicked through the aerial photographs. "He opened up the canopy for me. I was shooting into clear air. There, the string of colour—that's Yann leading his canoeists across the lake."

"It's an impressive shot," says Tor, smiling, and I'm filled with relief at his light heartedness. I suddenly realise how fortunate I am to have him in my life. I kiss him and stand up, heading toward the kitchen. From the hallway I call back, "I'll make us some Labrador tea."

I place the brown leaves into the filter. The tea brings back pleasant memories: the taste of pickerel on my lips, the wind in my hair at one thousand meters. I think about how Tor and I have been married for just over one month. I always assumed life would turn out wrong and when it didn't it amazed me, but what kind of luck did I give the people I loved when I always abandoned them? My parents raised my first child, and when I gave birth again at sixteen I gave the baby away. Everyone thought I was crazy not to have abortions, but I wanted to add life to the world. I also need to feel the world and the wind breezing by because it's the only thing that helps me forget the past. Yet I know that I have to learn to take fewer risks: a rabbit foot and not a wolf pelt.

At the airport I gave the wolf pelt to an old woman sitting alone. I only hope she didn't think that it was I who had killed and skinned the wolf. I'll always remember how she nodded, and in this one gesture said yes, and thank you. Or at least that's how I imagined it.

THILA VARGHESE

Thila Varghese lives in London, Ontario, where she works part-time during the academic year as a senior writing advisor at Western University. Her short story "*The Charcoal Marks*" was longlisted in the 2022 CBC Short Story Prize. Her translations of Tamil literary works have been published in international journals and magazines. One of her translations was shortlisted for the 2023 Armory Square Prize for South Asian Literature in Translation. As a freelance writer, Thila has contributed news and feature articles to publications in Red Deer and Ponoka, Alberta, as well as Fort Frances and London, Ontario.

* *Photo by Stefano Trulzi*

On the Edge of My Couch

Thila Varghese

The salesgirl behind the counter is sliding products across the scanner and bagging them with practiced efficiency, but every time she glances at me, I am panic-stricken. She knows what I'm up to. Maybe she knows where I live. Perhaps lives in the same neighbourhood.

"Ma'am, that is thirty-nine dollars and ninety-nine cents."

The salesgirl's loud, impatient voice interrupts my rapid succession of thoughts. Everyone waiting behind me in the long lineup at the drug store in the East End Mall seems to look at me with contempt. The sly looks and suppressed giggles. What did I do to deserve all this? What else ... old age, of course, and .... I fumble through the clutter in my purse to pay her. At least I wouldn't have to put up with this much longer.

I walk out of the drug store and across the food court to the ladies room at the northwest corner of the mall. It is empty. I take extra care removing the pills from the medicine bottle on the counter. A paper towel sheet will do just fine. I pull a sheet, and dropping the handful of pills on it, I quickly fold the sheet and slip it into my purse. I don't want to answer any questions from my daughter Rani, so I need to get rid of the bottle here. She's at Scissor's Palace, right next to the food court in the Mall, getting her hair done. I bend down to dispose of it in the garbage can nearby. As I turn to my left to pick up my shopping bag, I catch a glimpse of this person in the mirror. Surely it is not me, this shriveled little mannequin with sags, bags, wrinkles and all. I recognize only the clothes on this person — a pair of grey pull-on slacks and a pale blue knitted blouse that Rani bought for me and insisted on my wearing them for this outing.

Perhaps, if I scratch the mirror hard enough, I might discover once again, a young woman in a beautifully hand-crafted royal blue silk saree, rich with intricate designs woven into it by the crisscrossing golden threads. The red vermilion on her forehead, the long, braided hair bedecked with Madurai jasmine flowers, and the unique South Indian bridal jewellery speak volumes of the special day ... the wedding day ... my wedding day.

I close my eyes to savour this momentary vision to its fullest extent. I can hear the nadaswaram, the auspicious double-reed wind instrument, playing a familiar tune amid the rustling sound of silk sarees as women busily attended to receiving the guests. I remember the intoxicating fragrances of sandalwood paste and jasmine flowers. I can even recall the sensation of the gentle grip that spoke of budding love and desires as I was led by the hand ceremoniously around the holy fire by the man in silk dhoti, who vowed to spend the rest of his life with me. He did keep his promise made by the sacred fire. But now, I feel as though I am encircled by raging flames in a strange place, and I just don't know how to get out. This is why there are pills in my purse, an escape plan.

"Mom ... are you all right?"

It's my daughter. I try to pull myself together. Rani is here.

"Mom, I've been going in circles looking for you." Her forehead is wrinkled with worry. "Mom, are you all right?"

I detect concern in her voice. I really have to stop zoning out like this in public. She must find these lapses a real ordeal. I worry my children too much. Maybe they're right. Perhaps I should be put away in a 'safe home.' I know that they have been contemplating this idea for quite some time now. I am old, but not senile yet. There are hints, you know — the pampering and the extra attention Rani has been showering on me lately during her days off work and the increasing number of phone calls from my son in Ottawa.

"Yes darling, I'm fine."

I look at her fondly. She is too young to understand that when one reaches my age, memories flow in unbidden, sometimes to keep company and sometimes to torment. A part of me sinks when I look at Rani, and I really have to struggle hard to recognize my own flesh and blood inside that mauve skirt and matching blazer. It is also very disconcerting to note that the farther I continue to recede inward, the wider the distance between our two worlds appears to be and the deeper my sense of alienation even from my own offspring. The door opens; the ladies room is starting to get crowded.

"Shall we go?" Rani leads the way. I walk past women greeting one another in high-pitched voices. "Hi Marianne! How are you?" "How is Bob? Beautiful weather, eh!" Small talk. It totally drains me to engage in small talk these days. I detest it. It makes me feel as though I am playing a stage role and, as such, have to repeat carefully memorized lines while the growing chasm continues to widen between the pointless words and the mind that has gone into a deep slumber, bored stiff, totally ignoring the presence of the body.

In the parking lot, Rani arranges the shopping bags in the back seat and I make myself comfortable in the front seat.

"Mom, you didn't tell me how I look? How do you like my hairstyle? Cost me a fortune. But tonight Arnold wants me to look my best."

I vaguely remember Rani mentioning a company party for her husband's visiting CEO from the east. Arnold enjoys his position as the senior accountant in the company's western division and hopes to advance to a key executive level appointment at the corporate office in Toronto. I must say that I no longer have any reservations about their future together. Arnold is very caring, thoughtful, and articulate, and in his own persuasive way, he did convince Rani's father that he was the right man for our daughter. Mind you, I had grave misgivings about the whole thing in the beginning. "Mixed marriage? It won't work. They come from two different cultures. Colours don't blend in and transform into a magical display of wonder in real life as they do on canvas." I was so worried and distraught. Rani's father saw to it that I pulled through. My skepticism, however, soon proved groundless. Arnold has been extremely good to Rani, and I have absolutely nothing to grumble about.

"The hairstyle is very becoming, Rani. I like it very much. I bet Arnold will too."

She smiles, settling into the driver's seat.

"Thanks, Mom."

I try to recall in vain a similar conversation I might have had with my mother. I guess I never did.

We pass through Evergreen Drive. Bereft of their glorious fall leaves, a handful of maple trees on the sides of the road look like emaciated holy men with tangled-up knotty hair standing on one foot, totally lost in meditation. The luscious evergreen trees dancing proudly in the cold wind outnumber the maples and seem to resent their company. "What are you doing here? You don't belong with us."

Rani pulls into the driveway of the brick building located at the dead end of Bear Hills Boulevard.

My husband and I raised Rani and Shankar in this split-level brick house. They're gone now, living in their own homes. And it's been five years since my husband passed away. But I remain. I refuse to leave, to be in a new place, surrounded by new faces. I know it's coming, the day I'll be moved, but I cannot allow it. I won't.

Rani brings in the groceries, and I ease myself onto the edge of my couch.

"Leave the chicken on the counter, Rani. I'll marinate it for the Tandoori preparation tomorrow." I stand back up. "On second thought, leave it in the fridge. I'll take care of it later tonight. I'm so tired. I want to lie down for a few minutes."

I walk to the bedroom holding tight to my purse.

"Mom, don't strain too much. I'll bring plenty of food tomorrow. Oh, I'm so excited! Haven't seen Shankar and Seetha for nearly nine months!"

Shankar and his wife Seetha are coming home tomorrow. He phoned me last week to tell me he'd taken a week off from his job researching for a government agency to visit.

He is probably coming home to talk me into moving to Golden Grove Manor like his sister.

When my husband died, there were no loose ends in my life. But there was no focus, either. No sense of belonging to sustain me through the day. My eating habits and sleeping patterns turned erratic, and along the way, my health deteriorated to a point where I began to feel light-headed and disoriented frequently and even pass out at times. My concerned daughter sought medical help, and based on the doctors' advice and recommendations, she has been driving me to Golden Grove Manor to have me spend a couple of afternoons or a day every week at the senior's home to prepare me for the 'eventual transfer.'

"Mom, can I keep your purse on the night table?"

Rani is gently tugging the purse wedged between my arms and my chest. What is she trying to do? I remember the pills and panic, pulling back.

"Mom, you can't sleep with that thing."

She's right. I'm acting crazy. The look on her face confirms it. What's wrong with me? Acting like this, I'm going to let the cat out of the bag.

"Yes, please. I guess I'm pretty exhausted." I watch Rani place my purse by the side of the night lamp.

"Rest well, Mom. Don't forget to reheat the casserole in the microwave for supper.

I've added some extra curry in it for you. Arnold and I will pick Shankar and Seetha up at the airport tomorrow morning. I'm sorry I have to run now. I'll see myself out, Mom. Love you."

I hear the door shut behind her and Rani's car zoom away. I get up quickly. I'm too worked up to feel tired anymore. Sitting on the edge of the bed, I stare at my purse. Is it the right thing to do? It's been a long time since I had come to terms with the idea of what is right and wrong by compartmentalizing situations and decisions into those I can live with and those I cannot. I can certainly live with what I have decided to do. Can I, really? Ironic question! My hands are shaking as I pull out the folded paper towel sheet. Why am I trembling like this? Before I know it, I see little blue pills scattered all over the carpet. Clumsy me.

I go to the kitchen and get a small container. I pick up the pills and drop them in one by one.

A very long time ago when I was growing up in India, there was a tortoise that lived by the pond near our backyard. No one knew how old he was, but he was a delightful sight for the children in the neighbourhood, trundling across the shorelines until one morning, someone found him flipped on his back. It took three men to turn him back on his belly, but the tortoise lay motionless for a long time, though still breathing. The children were told to leave him alone because he was dying. When they finally buried him, I collected the smoothest pebbles I could find and laid them down, one by one, to form a circle around the burial spot.

I wonder how long the old tortoise had been struggling on his back before he finally gave up. In more ways than one, I have now arrived at that juncture. How long should I drag on with my failing health and why? I'm too tired to go on and too scared to contemplate the inevitable as I find myself receding helplessly further and further into the unknown. I need to get off the stage as quickly as possible while I still have control over that option. Little blue pills will put an end to all my anxieties and struggles in a peaceful eternal slumber. I haven't exactly decided on when I'm going to do it. Maybe the night before Shankar leaves — then he wouldn't have to make another trip for the cremation. He can say his final good-bye and go on with his life with Seetha.

Seetha, she reminds me so much of myself when I was her age. Rani is different. She was born and brought up in Canada. But Seetha, I brought her all the way from a small town near Madurai, where the rolling hills meet the luscious valley.

Following Rani's wedding, I told Shankar in no unmistakable terms that I would not go through another mixed marriage. His ailing father and I would make a trip to India that summer and look for a suitable bride and the marriage would take place in the fall. From that moment on, I moved ahead with my plans as though I was possessed. 'A good looking woman with traditional upbringing' was my only condition to the marriage broker. Seetha, the eldest with two younger siblings, came from a family that has been farming in the area for generations. Shankar married her without a murmur. If he had been entertaining any romantic notions of his own, he certainly did not verbalize them. Seeing my distress at Rani's wedding, he complied with my whims without a question.

Strange to say, the moment Shankar tied the knot on the nuptial thread around Seetha's neck, I was not sure whether I did the right thing. Poor Seetha! She looked so lost and out of place in that wedding crowd and at the reception we held in the evening.

What I had failed to take into consideration was the fact that Shankar and Seetha came from two different worlds despite their apparent common cultural background. Even when I reluctantly contemplated the issue after the fact, I tried to find comfort in the thought that Seetha would look after Shankar no matter what. I counted on her small town East Indian upbringing to keep them together as a unit. Still, sometimes I just can't get rid of the nagging question whether I had intentionally sought a subservient woman for a daughter-in-law who would exist only as Shankar's wife.

I place the container of pills on the night table and walk over to the kitchen through the long hallway. I prepare and pour the marinade made of yogurt and spices over the skinned chicken legs. Shankar loves tandoori chicken. Unlike Rani, he has an abiding taste for East Indian cuisine. Rani said that she'd bring plenty of food tomorrow, quite likely a sumptuous selection of eastern and western menu from Curry House. I can hardly visualize Rani slaving over a meal like I used to. Then again, Rani's world is not as narrow and limited as mine. I had never concerned myself with anything beyond the clearly defined boundary lines of my family. So, it is no wonder that the comforting familiar rhythm of my daily routine came to an abrupt end when Rani's father passed away.

At Golden Grove Manor, I tried, perhaps halfheartedly at first, but no matter how hard I tried, I wound up feeling like an overblown balloon about to burst. I got sick of 'putting my right hand in and my right hand out.' And I certainly didn't want to do the 'hokey pokeys.' I also couldn't stand what I had summarily dismissed as condescending compliments on my colour scheme every time I chose to dump some paint on my canvas during the art hour.

The long hours I had spent at the Manor have only intensified my anxiety. Why wouldn't my children recognize the obvious? I feel as though I'm forced to bid good-bye to my past, my heritage, and my roots, and play a final nerve-wracking role before I rest. That will be the real test, and I know I'll fail miserably. I wouldn't belong — not that I, being the first generation immigrant that I am, had ever deluded myself otherwise. I didn't have to consider any of this when my husband was alive. I belonged with him and nothing else had mattered.

In moments of despair, I had needed no spoken words for comfort. A gentle look or a hug from my husband had said it all. "It doesn't matter. I'm here for you. You belong." Rani's father was everything to me. Consequently, I still have a hard time managing the weight of his loss under which my whole world continues to crumble. Only Seetha could understand the depth of my feelings.

I am struggling to stay afloat in the middle of what appears to be a turbulent ocean. The shores are nowhere in sight and I am starting to sink. How did I get here?

The fact that I have nowhere to go became crystal clear to me during the trip I took to my home town in India three years ago. It was Rani who came up with the idea of the trip. But, travelling to India alone at my age with limited familiarity meant not only relying on others to get around but also coming face to face with what it means to be a widow in the family circle. The inevitable kaleidoscopic shifts in family relationships were not so subtle any more. Any romantic notions I might have entertained about the distant 'home' when my husband was alive came crashing down so fast. Stepping outside the increasingly suffocating circle, I could literally 'disappear' among the natives in the noisy, crowded bazaars in India and blend in without attracting attention, but I'm still a stranger there. I do not share their everyday struggles and joys and their moments of agony and glory. I have no natural inclination for the things that make them tick. It feels as though I have slept through a long journey and can't figure out where I have arrived at. My past has rejected me and my future continues to elude me. Where does a 'foreigner' belong? I can't go back to the country from where I had come. It is too late. My whole life seems like a jigsaw puzzle missing many crucial interlocking pieces. After raising two children in North America, I'm still an 'alien insider.' Back in the land where I was born, I have become a 'native outsider.'

I peer through the window. It is quite dark outside and the rain is pouring down in torrents. When Rani left, there was not a cloud in the sky. Strange weather. It is past eight o'clock. Should I reheat the casserole? I am not very hungry these days. I spend most of my time sitting on the edge of my couch, desperately trying to dissect and make sense of the thoughts cascading through my mind. Underneath it all, there is a constant feeling of living on borrowed time.

I wake up to the shrill sound of the telephone ringing. The feeble morning rays of the sun filtering through the relentless rain barely make it through the sheers to announce their presence. Rani's voice on the phone is shaky.

"Mom .... Mom ....." She is crying. There's so much background noise at the other end that I could barely hear her. I hear people talking and an unintelligible paging call competing with the distress sound of a baby crying.

"Rani, what's wrong? ...what's the matter? ... where are you?"

"Mom ... I don't know how to say this ... we're at the hospital…there ... there has been an accident .... slippery roads….a pickup truck veered off the lane …. car crash on Highway 2 near Leduc .... Shankar and Seetha...were thrown out of the car… no seatbelts… Shankar is gone .... and Seetha is injured badly …."

Rani is sobbing uncontrollably. Arnold takes over. He is begging me to be strong for Rani, and for Seetha.

Arnold's voice is slowly fading away until there is only silence. Shankar ... my little boy. I see him as a little boy in muddy baseball clothes and an eternal smile on his face.

I look out the window. My vision extends far beyond the close-cut lawn to the distant, misty prairie field. I see a little girl standing all alone and crying in the middle of the vast stretch of the boundless land. Looks like Rani, my little girl. I recognize the polka dot dress, her favourite. I race to the middle of the field and hug her close to my heart. I lift her tear-streaked face gently toward mine. It is not a little girl's face, not even Rani's face. It's Seetha. ...... Oh, what have I done?

I let go of the receiver. The little blue pills in the container by the side of the night lamp mock me.

Acknowledgements

Beyond Boundaries (2023) is the culmination of the inaugural Dave Williamson National Short Story Competition. These acknowledgements honour both the process of the competition and the celebration of its product.

A conversation between **Chris Hall** and **Joanna Graham** of **McNally Robinson** and **Alex Dawson** and **Sharon Hamilton** of the Manitoba Writers' Guild (MWG) in the spring of 2022 sparked the idea of departing from our quarterly short story contests. We all agreed that one major competition, with expanded outreach and larger prizes, might result in greater visibility for and interest in the MWG.

Volunteers from our Program Committee constituted the initial planning committee: **Danie Botha** (Chair pre 2022 AGM), **David Yerex Williamson** (Chair post 2022 AGM), **Alex Dawson**, **Andy Dutfield**, **Sharon Hamilton**, and **Susan Rocan**, plus former committee member **Anna Valdron**. Several early decisions were made that significantly influenced the subsequent scope and direction of the competition. The first was to "go national." This was huge. We were still in the process of making determined efforts to include and engage our northern, interlake, rural, and otherwise distant-from-Winnipeg writers in our programming. Somebody quoted Robert Browning's, "Ah, but a [person's] reach should exceed [their] grasp, or what's a heaven for?" and we thought, "What might that mean for our competition, for our members, and for writers in general?" A major consequence was to expand our reach to intentionally and specifically encourage entries from diverse cultures, races, gender identities, and ages. The second decision was to increase our prize money, which typically varied between $50 and $100 for one winner, to having three winners, each receiving a significantly larger prize ($1000; $600; and $400 respectively). The third was to find a way to compensate our judges, who would be playing a significant role in determining our winners. The fourth was to publish a collection of the winning stories, and the fifth was to find ways to pay for these plans! The sixth decision was to determine an honorary patron who would contribute the gravitas of a lifelong commitment to writing in the province.

Dave Williamson came to mind almost as soon as we began our discussions. Dave is a founding member of the Guild as well as the person who created, designed, and developed the highly respected Creative Communications program at Red River College Polytechnic (RRCP). He is also a well-known author who has nurtured aspiring writers for decades not only at RRCP but also in the acclaimed McNally Robinson Community Classroom. His national portfolio extends to his having served as President of the Canadian Writers' Union. Dave's gentle humility sparkled with an almost imperceptible frisson of excitement as he generously accepted our invitation.

As our plans developed, particularly with someone as experienced and revered as Dave Williamson, we knew we had to push ourselves to the limit to create not just another writing competition, but something very special to the community of writers in Manitoba and across Canada. And while our committee members and volunteers willingly donated their time, we knew we couldn't rely on entry fees alone to shape the kind of competition we aspired to create. We had no idea how many or how few entries we would receive. Almost spontaneously, several members offered to donate not only expertise but also cash to the project. We acknowledge the sincere generosity of **Danie Botha**, **Andy Dutfield**, **Sharon Hamilton**, **Kamal Malaker**, **Anna Valdron**, **Den Valdron**, **Dave Williamson**, and **David Yerex Williamson**, whose contributions have been used to help with the printing of this volume.

The decision to 'go national' by building on our connections with other provincial and territorial Guilds had certainly broadened our outreach, as had our decision to engage our northern and rural communities more actively. Then, serendipitously, the **Manitoba Arts Council** announced a grant for competitions within the arts community. We are grateful to **Sylvie Côte**, Guild member and volunteer, for taking the lead in preparing this grant application. It provided the much-needed safety net to fund the prizes for the winners.

Being awarded the grant was exciting, but its cash value was only the beginning of its benefit to the Manitoba Writers' Guild. During the process of assisting Sylvie with the grant, I studied the assessment criteria by which we would be judged and discovered that the Council was looking for far more than a straightforward competition. The Manitoba Arts Council would be scrutinizing and evaluating how the competition would further our vision, mission, and goals (VMGs), the heart of which is to embrace, support, and nurture all Manitoba writers. We had not specifically referenced them in any of our discussions. Nor had we connected VGMs explicitly to our competition in our grant application. Starting from that moment of realization, we centred our subsequent planning around the concept of inclusion and support. One example of this change is that, throughout Manitoba and across most of Canada, our planning team and promotional team (**Lori Gaudet**, **Katherine Westwood**, **Alyssa Gallano**, and **Nathalie Kaboha**) sent invitations to organizations and community groups that represented the broadest range of diverse cultures, races, religions, gender identities, and ages. These lists of groups, totalling well over 600 organizations, were collated primarily by **Alex Dawson** with assistance from **Susan Rocan** and distributed by **Carrie Hatland**, **Andy Dutfield**, **Susan Rocan**, **Alex Dawson**, **Anna Valdron**, and **Sharon Hamilton**.

A writing competition cannot occur without well-qualified judges. Our preliminary judges, **Barbara Becker**, **Harry Hobbs**, **Pat Stephanchuk**, **Jennifer Tesoro**, **Andrea Von Wichert**, **Glenda Walker-**

Hobbs, and **Judy Williams**, undertook the gargantuan task of reading the 96 stories submitted to the competition, checking them for compliance with the guidelines, looking at basic issues of grammar and punctuation, elements of fiction, and effectiveness of storytelling to select the top 26. Our lead judges (**Raye Anderson**, **Bob Armstrong**, **Zilla Jones**, and **Frances Koncan**) then took over the task of reading for deeper issues of dynamics among plot, character, setting, and theme, pacing, and, once again, the overall effectiveness of storytelling to settle on our three winners and our honourable mentions. All judging decisions throughout the competition were based on blind-judging. Not until after the winners and honourable mentions were decided did the judges receive information about author identity or place of residence.

All of which brings us to this volume, Beyond Boundaries. **Lori Gaudet**, well-known throughout the Guild for designing and editing our bi-monthly newsletter and MailChimp mailouts, led a team of volunteers to edit the manuscripts and make this book ready for printing by **PrintPro**. Special mention also goes to **Katherine Westwood** for designing the splendid cover and to **Den Valdron** for his publishing advice and legal support.

Stewarding finances that included almost 100 entry fees, several donations, and our Manitoba Arts Council grant required meticulous attention to detail. **Clarice Sinohin**, our treasurer, works quietly behind the scenes but consistently oversees and balances income and expenses with accuracy and integrity.

Finally, I'd like to acknowledge the compassionate leadership and reliable support of **Andy Dutfield**, President of the Manitoba Writers' Guild and Chair of the Board of Directors.

Sharon Hamilton
Organizational Manager of the Dave Williamson National Short Story Competition
Vice President of the Manitoba Writers' Guild

* *Photo by Angelique Duseigne*

LEAD JUDGES

*In alphabetical order by last name.

Bob Armstrong

Bob Armstrong is a Winnipeg novelist, short-fiction writer, speechwriter, writer of environmental impact reports, book news columnist and aspiring comedian. His second novel, *Prodigies* (Five Star/Cengage) was co-winner of the 2022 Margaret Laurence Prize for Fiction in the Manitoba Book Awards and his first, *Dadolescence* (Turnstone), was shortlisted for the best first book award in Manitoba. His short fiction and creative non-fiction have been published in Prairie Fire, The Fiddlehead, Exile, FreeFall, anthologies of speculative fiction and comedy and other places.

* *Photo by Rosemary Szabadka*

Raye Anderson

Raye Anderson is a Scots Canadian who taught Drama and ran Theatre and Community arts programs for many years, notably at Prairie Theatre Exchange in Winnipeg, in Ottawa, and Calgary.

Raye has been a resident of the Interlake since 2007 and presently lives in Gimli. Her first crime fiction novel, *And We Shall Have Snow*, was published by Signature Editions in 2020. It was a finalist for Best First Novel for the Crime Writers of Canada, Awards of Excellence and was also shortlisted in the Original Softcover Fiction category of the WILLA Literary Awards.

The second book in the series, which features Sergeant Roxanne Calloway of the RCMP, occurs mostly in Winnipeg, in a fictional theatre company. Titled *And Then Is Heard No More*, it was published in 2021, and was the Winnipeg Free Press/McNally Robinson Book Club pick for July/August of 2022.

Raye returned to the Interlake as the setting for her third book, *Down Came The Rain*, published by Signature Editions in 2022. The fourth in the series, *Sing a Song of Summer*, will be released this spring.

* *Photo by Kayla Gordon*

Zilla Jones

Zilla Jones, she/her, is an African-Canadian writer living on Treaty 1 territory (Winnipeg.) She is a 2023 Journey Prize winner and has also won the Malahat Review Open Season award, Jacob Zilber award, Freefall short prose award, and GritLit festival award. She placed second in the Prairie Fire and Austin Clarke fiction prizes, and received Honourable Mention in the Room magazine short story contest. She has also been longlisted twice by the CBC short fiction prize and was a finalist in the Alberta Magazine Publishing awards. Her work appears in *Prairie Fire, the Malahat Review*, *Prism International*, *Freefall*, *the Fiddlehead*, *the Puritan*, *Room*, and *The Journey Prize Stories*. Zilla is also a busy criminal defence and human rights lawyer, anti-racism educator, singer, and mother to musical and athletic children.

** Photo by Ian McCausland*

Frances Konkan

Frances Koncan (she/they) is an Anishinaabe and Slovene playwright based in Treaty 1 territory on the land currently known as Winnipeg, Manitoba. Originally from Couchiching First Nation, they hold a BA in Psychology from the University of Manitoba and an MFA in Playwriting from the City University of New York Brooklyn College. They are currently the Writer-in-Residence at the Winnipeg Public Library. As a playwright, their work includes: *Women of the Fur Trade*, *Space Girl*, and *zahgidiwin/love*.

* *Photo by Ady K Photography*

PRELIMINARY JUDGES

*In alphabetical order by last name.

Barbara J Becker

Barbara J. Becker, linguistic consultant, is the editor of three Winnipeg Best Seller, *Measured Words* anthologies. Barbara has written and published short stories, poetry, and creative non-fiction. She has worked as a forensic linguist, and has facilitated creative writing workshops. She is a member of the Manitoba Writers' Guild.

* *Photo by Jay Gaune Photography*

Harry Hobbs

A retired librarian, Harry Hobbs has lived in Flin Flon for forty-six years. He is involved in Toastmasters, Flin Flon Writers Guild, and in Literacy. He is a lay preacher at the Lutheran Church and does services at the local nursing homes and meditations on local radio. He has published two novels, short stories and poems in various anthologies, co-authored a book on Flin Flon with wife Glenda, and edited a book of children's poetry. He was chosen to be a participant in the Royal Bank Emerging Arts program. His Christmas nativity play was performed by a local church Sunday School. He has been a facilitator for poetry and fiction courses at Writers Village University, of which he has been a member since 1998. Both Harry and Glenda have been very involved for the past twenty-one years of organizing a community poetry reading in Flin Flon.

Pat Stefanchuk

Pat Stefanchuk is a retired educator who taught elementary grades for eight years before teaching elementary music for ten years. After getting her Masters in Education degree, she became the Arts Consultant for Seven Oaks School Division in the 1980's. She took on the role of Vice Principal at Ken Seaford Middle School for five years and finally served as principal of Margaret Park Elementary School for nine years. She enjoys belonging to a writers' group, serving on the Seven Oaks Education Foundation, visiting her son and daughter-in-law in Florida and attending many concerts and plays with her daughter during the winter months.

* *Photo by Richard LyonsPhotography*

Jenn Tesoro

When Jenn Tesoro is not writing herself, she enjoys thinking about writing, reading other people's writing, and contemplating the true power of the pen in today's dynamic and unexpected world. Jennifer is currently pursuing a doctorate in Peace & Conflict Studies, and has received her Master's degree from the University of British Columbia in Adult Learning and Global Change, and two undergraduate degrees in Psychology and Education. Prior to her doctoral pursuits, she was a practitioner in international education leadership, and had the pleasure of living, working and writing in Vienna, Kazakhstan, Istanbul, and Bangkok. On prairie snowdays, she enjoys spending time with her daughter, listening to vintage vinyls, and dreaming about pelicans landing against the running water currents.

* *Photo by Dave Swiecicki*

Andrea Von Wichert

Andrea von Wichert is a writer/performer/visual artist working in Treaty One Territory. Her latest performance "*TRIGGER WARNING: Cassandra*" was produced by SICK+TWISTED Theatre Company.

** Photo by Leif Norman*

Glenda Walker-Hobbs

Glenda Walker-Hobbs (Glennis Hobbs) is a Canadian poet and writer from Flin Flon. She graduated from University of Winnipeg with her B. A. degree. She helped found a local Writers Guild and currently serves as its secretary. She is a long-time member of Writers Village University and co-moderator of Word Weavers Poetry Group as well as belonging to an international poetry group that meets online. She has achieved her Certificate in Creative Writing and is working on her MFA in Poetry. She worked in the Manitoba Writers Guild Apprenticeship with George Amabile. She has published thirteen books of poetry, including seven chapbooks and has had prose and poetry published in various anthologies and e-zines including Village Square.

Judv Williams

Judy Williams is a community builder, social worker and policy analyst with the Province of Manitoba. She is a board member of the St. Norbert Arts Centre (SNAC) and a co-chair of the SNAC mentorship program and GerryFest, an annual event that supports artists (writers, visual artists, and performers of various genres) from communities underrepresented in artistic sectors with professional mentorships. Judy is often invited by groups to present on her family's Black Canadian experience and history, which is the focus of her current research and writing. She is an active volunteer of the Manitoba Writers Guild.

www.ingramcontent.com/pod-product-compliance
Lightning Source LLC
LaVergne TN
LVHW012059160826
845678LV00014B/2878